T0265703

THE INCONVENIENT GERMAN

THE INCONVENIENT GERMAN

Peter Steiner

SEVERN
HOUSE

First world edition published in Great Britain and the USA in 2022
by Severn House, an imprint of Canongate Books Ltd,
14 High Street, Edinburgh EH1 1TE.

Trade paperback edition first published in Great Britain and the USA in 2023
by Severn House, an imprint of Canongate Books Ltd.

severnhouse.com

British Library Cataloguing-in-Publication Data
A CIP catalogue record for this title is available from the British Library.

ISBN-13: 978-1-4483-0641-1 (cased)
ISBN-13: 978-1-4483-0648-0 (trade paper)
ISBN-13: 978-1-4483-0649-7 (e-book)

All Severn House titles are printed on acid-free paper.

Typeset by Palimpsest Book Production Ltd.,
Falkirk, Stirlingshire, Scotland.
Printed and bound in Great Britain by
TJ Books, Padstow, Cornwall.

For Jane

PART ONE

Lucky Charlie

There was an explosion, a jolt that snapped Charlie's head back, and the Mustang shuddered and pitched. The stick went wobbly, and the plane rolled belly up and burst into flames. Captain Charlie Herder ducked his head, pulled the red handle, and the canopy blew off. He released the safety harness and dropped out into the night sky. He pulled the cord, and the parachute opened with a jerk.

He heard the roar of the bombers and fighters above him, heading home. To his west, Munich was on fire. Looking down, he saw nothing but black. Charlie wished he had paid better attention in Miss Kitzmann's German class. You think of funny things in moments like this.

He recognized the smell of fresh-mowed hay as the ground came up to meet him. He landed hard. The chute settled softly over him like a shroud. Charlie lay still for a moment, then pushed it aside. When he stood, he felt a sharp pain in his hip. His shoulders and arms hurt too, but when he moved around a little more, it was all right.

The sky above the woods glowed red. Charlie gathered up the chute and headed for the trees. It was just getting dark, and he had maybe six hours until first light. Whenever a plane went down, you knew there would be German patrols out looking for the crew.

Charlie stuffed the chute under the trunk of a fallen tree and covered it with forest debris. He set out along the edge of the woods. He had seen the Mustang crash in a ball of flame, and he needed to find a hiding place as far away as possible. The woods ended at a dirt road. He followed the road for a while over gently rolling terrain. There were more woods on his left and fields on his right. He came to a three-sided shed. A pipe out front dripped water into a wooden trough. Inside the shed, he found rakes and forks and a few other tools. Maybe he could stay here for a while.

Charlie was about to drink when he heard men's voices coming his way. There was a tiny loft under the shed's roof, and Charlie climbed the small ladder and pulled it up after him. He lay flat on the floor. Mice scurried to get out of his way.

When he was in intel, Charlie had interviewed pilots who made it back. They all said being taken by German soldiers was your best bet. They might rough you up a little, but they wouldn't hurt you too bad. You'd end up a POW. Civilians were riskier. More than one captured pilot had been killed by an angry German mob.

The soldiers down below were nervous. One kept making jokes nobody laughed at. They were probably clerks and cooks and mechanics. They figured that somewhere nearby a desperate pilot was waiting to cut their throats. They held their rifles ready and peered into the darkness all around. Their radio came to life and caused them to go quiet.

'*Scheiße!*' said the joker. Charlie knew what *Scheiße* meant. When you took German, the cuss words were the first ones you learned.

A command came from the radio.

'*Jawohl, Herr Leutnant!*' said the radioman, trying to keep his voice low.

The lieutenant said something else. He sounded impatient.

'*Nein, Herr Leutnant.*'

The lieutenant said something else.

'*Ein Mustang P-einundfünfzig.*' P-51. Charlie understood that. They were talking about his plane.

'*Zwei kilometer,*' said the man, and then something else Charlie didn't catch.

The lieutenant said something else.

'*Jawohl, Herr Leutnant.*' The men finished smoking. The butts hissed as they dropped them in the trough. The men shifted their rifles and left the way they had come. Charlie could hear them for a while, a muttered curse here, a cough there, then silence.

Charlie had considered surrendering to the soldiers. He had almost called out to them as they were leaving. But better, he thought, to surrender in daylight where they could see him clearly, hands raised, no nasty surprises. He was likely to end up a prisoner of war. *But what's the hurry?* he said to himself.

He decided they wouldn't be back this way again. This was as good a place as any to get a couple of hours of sleep. He lay back and fell asleep almost immediately.

Something woke him suddenly. He couldn't tell whether it was something he heard or dreamed. After waiting a while, he climbed down from the loft and took a deep drink from the pipe. The water was cold and good. The metal was cool against his cheek. It reminded him of Ohio and his granddad's farm.

The first light showed gray on the horizon. Charlie set out and walked until he came to a paved road. A milestone said, *Otterfing, 8 km.*

The Apricot Tart

Charlie kept to the woods as best he could. It didn't seem that difficult; much of Bavaria was woods. Later that morning, Charlie came to what looked like a forester's cabin. He watched from the trees for a long time. There were no signs of life. When he approached the house, chickens that had been sleeping started squawking and running about. Charlie ducked back into the trees and waited. Nobody came out.

The cottage was locked tight. The windows were heavily shuttered, and the doors were solid oak. There was no getting in. A pair of overalls was hanging on a clothesline. In a shed behind the cottage, Charlie changed his uniform pants for the overalls and put on a canvas coat he found hanging there over his sheepskin. A bag of walnuts hung from a hook in the shed, and Charlie filled his pockets. There was a small garden with spinach, lettuce, and radishes, and he ate some of each.

Charlie walked through the forest all day, following trails and timbering roads, always heading southwest as best he could, not with any goal in mind, other than putting distance between himself and the downed Mustang. He was hungry and regretted not killing a chicken. He had seen it done often enough at home.

He came to a river, the Isar maybe. He remembered the Isar from the briefing maps. He turned south and stuck to the riverbank as best he could. He came upon a small rowboat hidden among the reeds. But there were no oars. The opposite bank was built up with what Charlie guessed were fishing huts. Beyond the huts were houses and a church steeple sticking into the air. People were home; Charlie smelled their fires.

Where there was a village, there was likely to be a bridge, and, sure enough, another kilometer upstream he came to a pretty stone bridge. He watched the occasional farm wagon cross while he waited for dark. *Wackerzell am Perz*, said the sign. So the Perz River, wherever that was, and not the Isar. The streets of the town were deserted. The town was blacked out. There was no moon.

The National Air Raid Protection League (the RLB) had appointed wardens in every German city and town, even small ones like Wackerzell. Hartmut Mueller, the mayor of Wackerzell, was also the town's warden, and being a man who loved order and regulations, he was out patrolling in his helmet and RLB armband. Even the smallest sliver of light showing would cause him to rap on the door and admonish whoever answered for being lax in their patriotic duty.

Wackerzell had fewer than a thousand people. The only industry was a family-run sawmill. There were no dams, no railroads, no transportation hubs, no roads or bridges of importance. The only way an air attack was coming to Wackerzell was by accident. But Hartmut Mueller insisted that, for the sake of the Reich's absolute security, no light must be allowed to escape into the night from Wackerzell.

Tonight, once again, Heinz Ulbricht the baker had light showing. Like all bakers, Heinz baked at night, and sometimes he opened the back door a crack to let out the heat. The door opened into a vestibule and from there on to a small, enclosed courtyard behind the bakery. A gigantic chestnut tree spread above the courtyard. Whatever light had spilled from the door was unlikely to be seen from 10,000 feet. But rules were rules.

Charlie was watching from the shadows. He was hungry enough that the smell of baking bread had drawn him too close. Other than walnuts and a few garden greens, he hadn't eaten anything since the previous day. The mayor handed the baker a citation and then turned on his heel and left, followed by the baker's curses. Heinz went back inside and slammed the door. Dawn was breaking as he came back out, carrying a basket of loaves to deliver to the grocery store.

Charlie was immediately inside. The smell of freshly baked bread almost made him dizzy. He tucked two loaves under his arm and was about to leave when he found an apricot tart. He grabbed it and hurried out of the door. Charlie retreated to an abandoned hut on the riverbank behind the sawmill. He ate most of one loaf and the entire apricot tart. He drank from a bottle of water.

Charlie fell into a deep sleep. He dreamed he was flying the Mustang upside down, surrounded in the cockpit by a sumptuous feast: his mother's fried chicken, mashed potatoes, collard greens, and an apricot tart.

Was Machen Sie Da?

C harlie had survived one day and two nights on the ground. He hadn't seen any German soldiers since that first time. He knew he was leaving a trail of thefts behind him. Still, getting caught began to seem less inevitable, and surrendering less appealing. He wanted to continue west to France. He figured the border would be heavily patrolled. Still, if he made it, he could link up with the French resistance. Quite a few pilots found their way back to England with the help of the French.

For now, though, he needed provisions. He needed food and water, of course. He needed rain gear – the sky was looking ominous. A rucksack of some sort would be good, a map for sure, a compass, and a knife if possible. Clothes were the easiest to come by. Every household hung out laundry. They also put their bedding in open windows each morning to air out, so their houses were wide open. Finding the map would be trickier.

Charlie staked out a house at the edge of the village close to the woods. There was a quilt airing in the window. He watched a young woman leave the house carrying a cloth bag and a basket. She got on a bicycle and pedaled off down the road. Charlie pushed the quilt aside and climbed in. In a cupboard, he found an oilskin jacket, a felt rain hat, a wool sweater. He went into the kitchen and found some canned sardines. He took a kitchen knife. When he laid the things on a chair and turned to explore the rest of the house, he found himself facing a round-faced boy of about six and his little sister. They regarded him with wide eyes.

'*Was machen Sie da?*' said the boy.

'*Ja, was machen Sie da?*' said the little girl, mimicking her brother and clutching his hand.

Charlie grabbed the things and fled back through the bedroom, out of the window, and into the woods.

Charlie moved southwest and acquired what he needed day by day. He avoided villages when he could, trying to steal what wouldn't be missed from isolated farms or forest cabins.

In a hiking hut, he found a rucksack hanging from a peg. It was filled with provisions. Charlie guessed it belonged to the hiker he met a little further along the trail. '*Grüß Gott!*' said the man. Charlie nodded and kept moving. The hiker didn't recognize his own rucksack, but he did notice there was something odd about Charlie and stopped to watch him go.

The next day, Charlie got lucky and found a map and a full picnic basket on the front seat of a beer truck while the driver and his girlfriend were having sex in the woods. That afternoon, he ate black bread, chicken, sausage, pickles, radishes, and washed it all down with beer. *This is almost too easy*, he thought.

A bicycle would get him to the border faster; later that day, he stole one. He pedaled west on narrow roads and was making good time. He encountered only one car and two tractors. The trouble was the roads were so narrow they had to slow to a crawl to pass him. Which meant they got a good look at him. In these parts, everyone knew everyone, and nobody knew Charlie. He abandoned the bicycle in the weeds and left the road.

Charlie had seen road signs with a red border and the word *Achtung!* beneath the black silhouette of a tank. And once, in a great pine forest, he came upon a cleared strip of land with five strands of barbed wire strung between tall concrete posts. There were signs every ten meters or so that said *Zutritt verboten. Lebensgefahr*. Entry Forbidden. Mortal Danger. He made a note on his map.

The next morning, as he was passing through Heidenried, a village of a dozen houses, he met the Wehrmacht face to face. He wanted to cross a river – the Fahle, his map told him. He didn't see a soul. He was halfway across the bridge when he heard the unmistakable rumble of tanks behind him. At the end of the bridge was a wheelbarrow, and Charlie picked it up and pushed it along as though he were working. As the tanks passed, the ground shuddered beneath him. The Panzer commanders stood tall in the hatch. They didn't even look at Charlie. They were too busy negotiating the narrow bridge.

There was now a small stack of police reports documenting Charlie's activities. The woman with two children had told police that a man had broken into her house. Her precocious six-year-old even described Charlie well enough – the sheepskin leather jacket had struck his fancy – to suggest to the authorities that the intruder could be an English or American pilot. The baker hadn't noticed that two loaves of bread were missing, but the tart was another story. It had been a special order for which the customer had supplied the eggs and butter herself. She was furious. The baker told the police, although he tried to blame the mayor for distracting him and causing him to leave the door unlocked. The bicycle had been reported stolen, too.

The lovers did not report the stolen picnic basket. Her husband was just back from the war, minus a hand and an eye. She imagined he had followed them, spied on their lovemaking, and taken the basket as a warning. Her lover said she was being ridiculous. He tried to convince her that it was some itinerant tramp. She said this was a sign that they should stop their affair. She cried. He became impatient and hit her. With a black eye, she had no choice but to confess to her husband. She expected to be beaten again. Instead, he took her to the police station, where she filed a complaint against her lover. It turned out she wasn't the first woman he had hit.

The Warden

The sirens started their desperate wail. The roar of hundreds of approaching bombers rattled the china and caused the curtains to flutter. Willi Geismeier and Lola Zeff left their apartment and locked the door. People came out of every apartment and ran down the stairs. Munich was being bombed nearly every day now. You came to expect it, but it never got easier.

'Keep moving, hurry up. Keep moving. Hurry up. This way.' Adolf Jobst, a boy of nineteen, was the building's official air-raid warden. It was his job to get everyone safely to the cellar. His helmet was too large and wobbled on his head. His eyes swam behind large eyeglasses. He had the faintest suggestion of a blond mustache. He looked like the science student he would have been in better times.

The Borskis were the last to come down. They lived on the second floor, but they were in their eighties, and stairs were difficult. Adolf waited for the Borskis even when the planes were overhead and the bombing had started. He sent Herr Borski ahead, closed the iron cellar door behind him, and took Frau Borski by the arm down the steep stone stairs.

Number 120 Drehfelderstraße had 139 residents in sixty apartments. Adolf lived with his sister Frieda on the fifth floor in what had been their parents' apartment before they were taken away by the Gestapo. Willi and Lola lived across the hall. Lola greeted Adolf as they passed. Adolf put his heels together and bowed his head sharply. 'Frau Meier,' he said. 'Herr Meier.' Walter and Inge Meier were the names Willi Geismeier and Lola Zeff went by these days.

The cellar was a low-ceilinged, cavernous space. It had a packed earthen floor, massive stone walls, and heavily timbered ceilings. The few dim electric bulbs did not quite illuminate the space. Adolf went around and lit a few kerosene lamps for when the lights went out. Willi and Lola found their place and stood leaning against the wall. There were no assigned places, but everyone returned to where they had gone the last time. The Borskis sat on a wooden crate. No one spoke. Everyone had learned to tie handkerchiefs or dishtowels over their mouths and noses.

You could hear the muffled roar of the planes and the thump of the artillery trying to shoot them out of the sky. The first bomb landed nearby. The electric lights went out, and a shower of debris fell from between the timbers. After a few seconds, the lights came back on. The air was filled with fine dust.

'Was that Dornier?' someone said. Dornier was the airplane works a kilometer away. Several people from the building worked at Dornier.

'A direct hit?' said someone else.

'For somebody,' said somebody else.

Now there were more bombs. The earth shook, and one of the kerosene lamps fell over and went out. A curtain of thunderous noise seemed to sweep through the cellar, a monstrous and fearsome vibration that made people cry out. Someone started to pray.

It was not Adolf's duty to do so, but he circulated through the space, offering reassurance and comfort as best he could. All he could do was remind people that courage helped, and this would end one way or the other.

Something enormous collapsed somewhere above them, causing the ceiling to tremble and another huge shower of dust to cover them. The building creaked and groaned. The air got thick and difficult to breathe.

Then it was over. The all-clear sounded.

Adolf climbed the stairs, was able to open the door, and went out. When he came back after a few minutes, it was with assurances that the building was intact. And so were the buildings on either side and across the street.

Everyone filed out of the basement, some climbing straight back up to their apartments, not wanting to see outside. Others went into the street to survey the damage.

They looked up at their building, shaking their heads in astonishment, pointing down the block at the mountain of bricks and cement spilling into the street. There would be people trapped in the cellar or dead. In the other direction, the facade of 195

Drehfelderstraße had been sheared off. Two streets over, several buildings lay in ruin. Someone remarked on what good solid German construction 120 Drehfelderstraße was. The bombing had been a catastrophe, but they could feel proud that good old 120 had withstood the attack.

The Aftermath

When the building down the street had collapsed, the weight of it had crushed part of its cellar. Willi and Lola joined the line of wardens, civil defense forces, and neighbors carrying away debris. You could hear the cries of those trapped in the rubble. After much work, they pulled the first survivors from the wreckage. One after another, they came out. First a bewildered child, then a woman clutching her broken arm, then an elderly couple who reminded Willi of the Borskis. As a tunnel into the cellar was enlarged, more people emerged, many injured, others just dazed or frightened, all of them coated in gray dust. Some volunteers ventured in to find those who couldn't come out on their own.

That evening, when Willi and Lola returned to their apartment, they found everything as they had left it. A couple of pictures were crooked, and a glass had fallen into the sink and broken. But there was no serious damage. They ate supper – pea soup, black bread, schmalz, and beer. They ate in a silent state of wonder.

Lola spoke first. 'Will they be back?' She meant the bombers.

'I'm sure they will,' said Willi. 'Dornier is still there. Munich is still there.'

'Listen,' said Lola. The sirens coming and going were almost constant. 'It sounds pretty bad,' she said. Once in a while, a dull thud rattled the windows. Somewhere a bomb had been triggered or a building had come down.

'Let's go to the garden tomorrow,' said Willi, looking for something hopeful to do. Three weeks earlier, they had planted vegetables in an allotment by the railroad tracks, and the spring's first greens would be ready to pick, as long as the garden was still there.

There was little food to buy in the city. Meat was rare, even on the black market. People kept rabbits in their apartments. *Balkonschweine* – balcony pigs – they called them. Willi wouldn't eat a rabbit, at least not one he had raised. Willi and Lola got eggs and butter, fruits and vegetables from friends in the country, and greens from the garden, so they weren't starving.

Germany was a mess. The Russia campaign was a disaster; a million German soldiers were already dead in the east. American and English bombers were coming every day from the west – a thousand bombers and a thousand fighters at a time. There were assassination plots, sabotage, anti-Hitler propaganda. The British and Americans had recently landed in Salerno in Italy and were advancing on Rome, and the Allies were getting ready to invade France.

Six months earlier, Willi and Lola would never have risked arrest by going out to help the way they had this afternoon. And they would never have dared to make a garden. Willi had been a troublesome policeman, even before Hitler had come to power, and had been kicked off the force. And since then, he had become even worse. He was a criminal and a traitor who had caused the death of two government higher-ups, a Nazi member of the Reichstag and a senior Gestapo officer. Lola was wanted because of her association with Willi. They had been in hiding for years, moving often, staying just ahead of the SS and police.

Lately, though, SS Captain Altdorfer, an admirer of Willi's, who made it his business to know such things, said the Gestapo had lost interest in Willi. And Detective Sergeant Hans Bergemann, a friend of Willi's still on the force, agreed with Altdorfer that Willi and Lola could move around a little more freely. As soon as he heard that, Willi had rejoined the underground operation he and Gerd Fegelein had started years earlier. Bergemann regretted having said anything, but that was the way Willi was.

The organization that the SS and the Gestapo referred to as the Flower Gang had started small when it became necessary to smuggle Lola out of Munich back in the thirties. She had gone to Fegelein's bicycle shop, and from there Pierre – a mysterious character no one knew anything about – drove Lola to Fedor Blaskowitz's house by Murnau where she could hide in relative safety.

Given the times and the urgent need, the Flower Gang had grown over the years. They were now providing false papers for Jews, resistance operatives, Allied pilots, anyone who needed their help, hiding them, escorting them to the border. No one knew how many they were, but they were all over Bavaria. Even Willi had no idea who they all might be.

A knock on the door this late in the evening made Willi jump. Lola went to the door while Willi went into the other room. It was Adolf Jobst, the young warden. He was still in his ill-fitting uniform, his face still dirty. He had just come in from helping dig out neighbors.

'*Guten Abend*, Herr Meier, Frau Meier,' he said, putting his heels together and nodding his head sharply in that little bow he been taught as a schoolboy. 'I'm sorry to disturb you so late. May I speak with you?'

Willi led Adolf to the kitchen table, and they sat down. Lola offered Adolf tea, but he declined.

'We have a thief, Herr Meier,' said Adolf.

'A thief?' said Willi.

'In the building, I mean. Someone is getting into people's apartments and taking things.'

'What things?' said Willi.

'Food,' said Adolf. 'Mostly food. During the bombings, when we're all in the cellar.'

'I see,' said Willi. He studied Adolf. 'And why are you telling me this?'

'Well, I don't know. I thought . . .'

'You should tell the police,' said Willi.

'Yes,' said Adolf. 'Yes, I know, but . . . I don't know, I thought you might be able to help.'

'What makes you think that?'

'I don't know. You seem to know a lot about . . . you observe things, people . . .' After a little more hemming and hawing, it came out that Adolf had figured out Willi had once been a policeman.

'How did he come up with that?' Lola wondered after Adolf had gone.

'I don't know,' said Willi. 'He's a bright kid. He pays attention. Bergemann came by once. Maybe he saw Bergemann. You just have to look at Bergemann and you know he's a cop.'

The Rhineland Bastard

Adolf thought anyone stealing food was probably hungry, and the police would treat a thief, even a hungry one, harshly. The trouble was Joachim Ballitz, who lived with his wife and son in a spacious apartment on the second floor, had had a big jar of *foie gras* and a bottle of French wine stolen. They had cost him a lot of money, and he wanted the thief punished.

'And it wasn't just wine,' said Ballitz. 'Chateau LaTour Pouillac,1922 is not just wine.'

Adolf just shrugged, which made Ballitz even angrier.

Herr Doktor Ballitz – he insisted on being called Herr Doktor – was the chief engineer at Dornier. He was a stickler for law and order, and a devout Nazi. He threatened to go to the police and file a complaint against Adolf Jobst if he didn't 'remedy the situation.' That Ballitz had bought the stolen goods on the black market didn't deter him from threatening with the police.

Adolf tried to explain to Ballitz that he was only the air-raid warden, but Ballitz didn't want to hear it. 'I was robbed of valuable goods,' he said, '*during* an air raid while you were in charge. Keeping the building secure during an air raid is part of your duty. Your sloppiness amounts to a dereliction of duty, and I demand that you find the thief and arrest them.'

Ballitz didn't stop there. He was sure he knew who the thief was. 'That . . . girl! Hanging around the building,' he said. 'I don't know why she's even still here. She should have been sent away with all the Jews and Gypsies.'

Black Africans had been coming to live in Germany from Germany's colonies – Togo, Cameroon, Southwest Africa – since the 1880s. They had never been welcomed into German society, and many Germans said now they should be 'dealt with' one way or the other. But Elke Oldenburg had been born in Germany. She was a German citizen by birth. Her father was Ibrahim Mbaye, a Senegalese officer in the French Army occupying the

Rhineland, and her mother was Anna Oldenburg, the daughter of the then-mayor of Dortmund. Ibrahim was an officer, tall and handsome in his uniform, with very black skin and large brown eyes. Anna was blue-eyed and apple-cheeked, with a cloud of wavy yellow hair. People stared when the two of them walked hand in hand through the streets of Dortmund.

The Treaty of Versailles was a war crime in Hitler's eyes, and that black soldiers were part of the army occupying the Rhineland added insult to injury. Hitler raged against the inevitable mixed-race children, like Elke, as a racial abomination. He said the Jews had arranged all this. They wanted the races to mix. Then these inferior children – 'Rhineland bastards,' he called them – would 'lower the German people's cultural and political level so the Jew could dominate.'

After his German tour of duty, Ibrahim Mbaye had returned to Senegal. Later, Anna threw Elke out of the house. It was the only way she could be reconciled with her own parents. Elke, still a teenager, found herself alone on the streets in a hostile land.

She left Dortmund and went south to the small city of Konstanz, a picturesque town on the Bodensee – Lake Constance – straddling the border with Switzerland. From her window, she could see border checkpoints, and beyond them freedom. She got to know the border and learned which guards were lax or indifferent or stupid. She didn't have identification, much less a passport. But she would slip over into Switzerland and back, just to know that she could.

Elke was beautiful. She was tall and slim, with coffee-brown skin, perfect teeth, striking blue eyes, and curly black hair she wore cropped short. In Konstanz, she fell in love with Egon Greiner, the drummer in a local jazz band. She eventually joined the band as the singer. They played every weekend at Die Laterne, where they did all the latest hits from America.

When the band broke up, Elke and Egon went to Munich. But in 1942, Heinrich Himmler ordered a census of African-Germans as the first step toward their eventual extermination. African-Germans were no longer allowed to work or even obtain residency permits. Elke wasn't allowed to stay anywhere legally. But the extermination never happened. There were just too few African-Germans to bother with.

Now Elke was on her own and was sleeping rough. She had met Adolf Jobst, the warden at 120 Drehfelderstraße, and he had offered her a tiny room under the basement stairs. In better times, the room had been for the building's resident handyman, but there was no longer a handyman. Elke scavenged a cot, a chair, a chest of drawers, a small table, a hot plate, a lamp, a few pans and dishes, and made herself a kind of home.

'I'm sure she's not stealing food,' said Adolf.

'How can you be sure?' said Willi.

Adolf explained that certain restaurants got special rations so that party members and military customers could count on a good *Tafelspitz* made with actual beef, or an apple strudel made with butter and slathered with whipped cream. Elke had learned that if she showed up at the back door of some of these kitchens at the end of the day, they would give her food, and plenty of it – uneaten courses, extra appetizers, desserts that otherwise would have been thrown away.

'How do you know this?' said Willi.

'Well,' said Adolf, his face turning red, 'sometimes she shares what she gets with Frieda and me.'

'Do you need food?' said Lola.

'No. Yes. Sometimes,' said Adolf. 'But we didn't ask for it. She says it's to pay for her room. Anyway, she doesn't have any reason to steal *foie gras* or fancy wine.'

Dandelion

Elke Oldenburg said that almost all the robbed apartments had been unlocked. 'Some people even leave their doors open they're in such a hurry. When the sirens start, everybody runs for their lives. People forget.'

'Do you know this or are you guessing?' said Lola.

'I know it,' said Elke.

They were sitting in her room beneath the cellar stairs, Elke on the edge of the bed, Lola on the wobbly chair. A narrow window under the ceiling let in a slanting ray of sunlight. 'I also know that Ballitz *didn't* forget,' said Elke. 'He has three locks on the door, and he locked them all.'

'How do you know?' said Lola.

'I saw him do it,' said Elke.

'Really?' said Lola. 'You were there?'

Elke just smiled and shrugged.

'If Ballitz was robbed . . .' said Lola.

'Then his son is the robber,' said Elke. 'Frau Ballitz went with Ballitz to the cellar; it has to be Dietrich. And Ballitz knows it.'

'You weren't in the cellar?' said Lola.

'No,' said Elke.

'So what!' said Dietrich when Adolf confronted him with the facts. Dietrich was normally a shy boy, and not stupid. But he hated his father and had relished taking his precious wine, which he seemed to love more than he loved Dietrich. Dietrich and his friends had popped the cork and passed the bottle around until it was empty.

Dietrich was fifteen and ran with a rough group, many of whom were living in bad circumstances – in ruined apartments, with drunken parents, or even on the street. Many had fathers who were away at war or already dead in Russia. Their mothers managed as well as they could, but with rationing, a housing shortage, no work, and now the bombing, they lived in desperation.

This gang – most of them still children – tried to support themselves and their families. They scavenged or stole what they could – food, clothes, ration cards, money.

While everyone was in the cellar and the bombs were falling and the building was shaking, Dietrich and a friend had taken as much food as they could carry to share among the gang members. And Dietrich took Ballitz's fancy food out of spite. He had stolen from his father before, but the *foie gras* and French wine were the last straw.

It wasn't much of a mystery or, given everything else that was going on, much of a crime. Willi suggested that Adolf post a notice in the foyer reminding everyone to lock their doors when they were out, even during air raids. He didn't think anything else was needed. Besides, people had to eat.

Early the next morning, Willi went downstairs and walked a designated route. He was startled to see that it was Elke Oldenburg who passed him the envelope. The Flower Gang was not detective work. But Willi thought it was important work, and it made use of his skills. It was as though all his earlier experience had been preparation for the required stealth and the danger.

When Colonel Rudolf Heinzl, who had passed top-secret documents to the British, came to Willi one day by way of Edvin Lindstrom at the Swedish consulate, Willi knew what to do and how to do it. The printshop he and Fegelein had set up years earlier provided Heinzl with false papers (he became Rudolf Gluecks). Two students – a young man and woman from Heidelberg – took Heinzl by train from Munich back to Heidelberg. Their papers were checked on the train without incident. From Heidelberg, they drove by car to Alsace where partisans walked Heinzl into France.

On a moonless night, he waited with a group of partisans in a pasture north of Lyon, staring into the black sky. A strong wind was at their backs. They saw the light blink three times just above the trees before they heard the plane's engine. They signaled with four blinks of a flashlight. Partisans at the sides of the improvised landing strip turned on their flashlights. The Lysander landed, bounced across the rough terrain, and stopped, and the lights went off.

Someone got out, carrying a satchel. Colonel Heinzl got in. The Lysander turned around, the flashlights along the strip were turned on again, and after a short taxi, the plane lurched into the air, heading for London.

A British SOE (Special Operations Executive) operative, who had parachuted into Germany, was moved around Bavaria for more than a month, keeping one step ahead of the Gestapo until he could finally be smuggled into France with the same two Heidelberg students getting him to the border. This time, though, someone identified the students. They were arrested by the Gestapo and tortured. But they gave up nothing, not even their own names. The Gestapo eventually found out who they were, but too late for it to be of any use.

Willi and Lola helped two RAF pilots, one after the other, to evade capture. They got the first one from Munich to Fedor's green house, where he stayed until he too could be moved into Switzerland and from there into France. He linked up with the resistance and was also eventually flown out on a secret Lysander flight.

The second one followed the same path two weeks later but was forced off track between the green house and the Swiss border. He got over the French border, which by now was trickier since it meant crossing the Rhine River. A guard at the electric works at the bridge by Müllheim got the pilot on to a coal car on its way back to France. The train stopped and started almost constantly to allow troop trains to pass, so the trip that should have taken six hours took two days. He caught a Lysander headed for London. The plane was shot up passing over Dieppe but limped home safely.

An American pilot and the German guiding him were not so lucky. They were caught crossing into France. The American was put in an OFLAG, a prisoner of war camp for officers. He escaped from that camp, was caught again, and sent to a different camp, where he stayed for the rest of the war. The German guide, himself a pilot who had lost an eye in an air battle and couldn't fly anymore, was sent to the concentration camp at Mauthausen, where he was forced to carry heavy blocks of stone up the so-called stairs of death over and over again until he was dead.

Several Jewish families got to Switzerland with help from the

Flower Gang. Others were betrayed along the way. The Gestapo was always lying in wait. And if the Gestapo caught you, they knew how to make you betray others. That is why it was important to know as little as possible about the mission, the operation, and the others involved.

As the organization grew, those in the network had taken on the names of flowers as code names. No one knew who came up with that idea. It might have been to honor the White Rose resistance, a group of Munich students who spread anti-Nazi propaganda and were executed in 1943. Willi was Dandelion.

The passports and identity cards in the envelope Willi was carrying had been manufactured across town. He was taking them to an apartment building in Neuhausen. Willi navigated his bicycle past the damaged train yards and the Dornier factory, which lay mostly in ruins. The local police station was also in ruins. Buildings everywhere were in various stages of destruction. The inside walls of rooms were revealed. Tattered wallpaper fluttered in the wind. A massive wardrobe, its doors flapping, teetered on the edge of what was left of a third floor, offering tantalizing glimpses of brightly colored clothes inside, until that tiny edge gave way as Willi rode past and the wardrobe tumbled end over end on to the pile of rubble below. Bodies were being pulled out of mountains of debris and lined up under sheets to be taken away.

As Willi arrived at his destination on a block completely unscathed – there were even pansies in flower boxes in some of the windows – he saw a parked car with two men inside. The men kept their eyes straight ahead. They were smoking. Men smoking in a car, he thought, are always up to something.

He carried his bike up the three front steps. He rang a bell and waited. He was buzzed in. Once inside, he waited. A voice at the top of the stairs said, 'Is that the mail so early?' He dropped the envelope into the small trash receptacle beside the mailboxes and said loud enough to be heard upstairs, 'In the Third Reich, the mail service is always improving.' He pushed his bike down the hall and out the back door. He rode down the alley and turned back on to the main street. The car with the two men was gone.

SS Lieutenant Laumann

S S Lieutenant Klaus Peter Laumann was from Prussia. He didn't like Bavaria. The Bavarian temperament was lax. The countryside, with its mountains and forests, was too voluptuous. The sing-song accent was annoying. The crucifixes at every crossroads were unsettling. Even after three months here, he kept his curtains closed so he wouldn't have to look at the Alps shimmering above him in the harsh southern sun. He had been stationed in Holland before and liked that better.

But before his arrival in Murnau, the SS detachment had been poorly managed, stymied by the Flower Gang's operations. The SS had no idea how many people were involved or even whether it was one operation or several. All they knew was that someone was helping Jews and others get out of the country. And it was happening right under their noses. The Gestapo had made two arrests, but without getting any useful information.

The two conspirators apparently hadn't known each other. 'Sunflower and Edelweiss,' said the sergeant. He had overseen their interrogation. 'They died without giving anything away.'

'Sunflower?' said Laumann.

'And Edelweiss. Code names,' said the sergeant.

'Their real names?' said Laumann. He leafed through the file.

'We never found out,' said the sergeant.

'You never found out their names? *Mein Gott!*' Klaus Peter Laumann had his work cut out for him.

He was puzzling over the few clues at his disposal when a small stack of reports landed on his desk. Most were petty crimes, and he marked the location of each with a pin on the wall map. He could see right away they had probably been committed by one person, an itinerant thief moving from up by Munich toward the southwest. He thought immediately of the downed American pilot who had avoided capture for a week now. It looked as if he was heading for the French border.

The pilot would need help once he got near the border. From all reports, the Flower Gang was in just that business. Laumann figured all he had to do was find the pilot and follow him until he linked up with the Flower Gang. Then he could deal with all of them at the same time.

He requested reports of any and all criminal activity, even breaking curfew or leaving curtains open during blackouts. He needed informers, and he needed them fast, and minor criminals were his best bet. Heinz Ulbricht, the baker who had violated blackouts, refused to cooperate, and when Laumann threatened him with some vague punishment for leaving his door open, Heinz was unfazed. Laumann figured he had nothing to offer and would only cause him trouble, so he let him go.

Egon Scharfheber, the man who had given his girlfriend a black eye, was a more promising prospect. For one thing, Scharfheber's job as a beer-truck driver took him all over Bavaria, giving him ample opportunity for all sorts of criminality, which Laumann could make use of. And he would be in a good position to collect useful information. More important, Scharfheber had been in trouble before.

Scharfheber was ushered into Laumann's office. The lieutenant glanced up and then went back to studying the file in front of him. For ten minutes, he turned the pages back and forth. Scharfheber shifted uneasily on his chair. He studied the Führer's picture hanging above the lieutenant. Finally, Laumann closed the file and slapped it with his hand, making Scharfheber jump. 'I see you like to beat up women.' Laumann held up a police photo of the girlfriend from the picnic. Her right eye was bruised and swollen shut.

'No, *Herr Leutnant*,' said Scharfheber, 'the judge dropped all charges. It was a misunderstanding. She . . .'

'Another misunderstanding, Herr Scharfheber?' said Laumann, holding up a photo of a different woman with a bruised face.

'I don't know her,' said Scharfheber. 'I've never . . .'

Laumann stood up, came around his desk, and hit Scharfheber hard on the chest, knocking him back in his chair. He stood over him with cocked fists, ready to hit him again. 'The Führer doesn't like men that hit women. And I don't either.'

Then his tone changed back to businesslike, as though nothing

had happened, like after a summer storm. 'Your work takes you
all over Bavaria, doesn't it, Herr Scharfheber, delivering beer to
hotels and inns and the like?'

'*Jawohl, Herr Leutnant,*' said Scharfheber, trying to sound
cooperative, while rubbing his chest where it hurt.

'You hear things from your customers and other people
you meet, don't you, Herr Scharfheber?'

'Hear things, *Herr Leutnant*? Please, I don't know what you
mean.'

'Well, you're on the road all day, you stay overnight in an inn,
you have supper there, hang out at the bar afterwards, talk to the
innkeeper, talk to other guests, about the war, about politics.'

'No, *Herr Leutnant*. No politics. I'm on the straight and
narrow path.'

'A party member?'

'Of course, *Herr Leutnant*.' he said, sitting up straighter.
'Absolutely.'

'But you didn't join until 1941.' Laumann read from a sheet
of paper he had taken from the file. 'A little late, wasn't it?'

Scharfheber said nothing.

The lieutenant took a step toward Scharfheber who leaned as
far back as he could, afraid he was going to get hit again. 'As
a loyal party member, Herr Scharfheber,' he said, giving the
word 'loyal' ironic emphasis, 'tell me, what do you think should
be the punishment for a truck driver who, say, sells stolen gasoline and meat out of the back of his beer truck?' He rattled the
paper and slapped it with the back of his hand, as if to say, *It
is all here on this paper*. The lieutenant was just guessing. But
a man like Scharfheber with a truck at his disposal was almost
certain to be doing some illegal dealing.

'No, no,' said Scharfheber. 'That's not true. Someone's lying.
Please, *Herr Leutnant*, you've got to believe me.'

'Don't lie to me, Scharfheber,' said the lieutenant, leaning
toward Scharfheber, his fists balled up. 'Don't you ever lie to
me.' He called to his assistant in the outside office. 'Sergeant!
Call the Gestapo to take this scum away.'

Scharfheber began to weep, then to plead. He wasn't in the
black market like some people. Never meat, never cigarettes. No,
none of that. Once he had sold a few liters of gasoline, once

some coffee. But that was all. Really. Only once. He was not that kind of man.

The SS lieutenant did not hit Scharfheber again. Instead, he studied him for what seemed like forever. 'You said you're "not like some people." What people would that be?'

'Just people, *Herr Leutnant*. People . . . I've heard about.'

'Go on,' said the lieutenant.

'A waiter,' said Scharfheber.

'Dammit, Scharfheber, you're trying my patience.'

'Sepp. I don't know his last name. At the Hotel zur Krone.' Scharfheber finally realized what the lieutenant was after. 'I'm on the road every day. I eat my supper at bars. I sleep in guest-houses all over Bavaria. People talk to me. They have forged ration cards. They buy and sell on the black market.'

Laumann did not call the Gestapo after all. He told Egon Scharfheber that it was his, Laumann's, mission to catch and liquidate a gang of smugglers and traffickers who were active in the area and were responsible for helping all sorts of human scum escape to Switzerland and France. Jews, enemy pilots, traitors – the worst of the worst. Egon Scharfheber could play a part in this effort, he could do the patriotic thing, or he could rot in prison. The choice was his.

Egon said he understood completely. He stood and saluted as best he could – '*Jawohl, Herr Leutnant.*' He left the lieutenant's office with a new assignment and a new lease on life.

Big Talk

The problem with Laumann's method was that the informers you recruited using threats and intimidation were almost certain to be unreliable. Sepp Krupke, the waiter, was pulled in by Laumann and, like Scharfheber, persuaded to join the team. But Krupke was no more trustworthy than Scharfheber.

Scharfheber was a braggart and a liar, and had soon told half a dozen people, including a barmaid he was trying to impress, that he was, as he called it, 'quasi-SS.'

'I can't tell you any more,' he said. 'It's top secret.' He even told Sepp Krupke he was on a special mission for the SS lieutenant. It didn't occur to Egon that Sepp might have been pulled in by Laumann by now and would figure out that it was Egon who had snitched on him.

Laumann brought Egon Scharfheber back after a couple of days to impress on him again what he expected and what would happen if he didn't come through. Scharfheber tried to invent a conspiracy on the spot: three men in a bar talking to one another in a low voice. They had mentioned the Führer's name.

'Are you joking, Scharfheber?' said Laumann. 'Stop the spy movie crap. Find something ordinary that is somehow out of place. An umbrella when the sun is out, that sort of thing. Or you'll find yourself in Dachau.'

'An umbrella?'

'Something in the wrong context, Scharfheber. Something that doesn't quite make sense, doesn't fit.'

Scharfheber was discouraged. He didn't get it. He understood that an umbrella on a sunny day was odd. But when he looked around, everything he saw seemed as it should be. He wondered if he would even notice if someone were carrying an umbrella when the sun was out. Maybe they just thought it might rain and had brought an umbrella along, or maybe they didn't like the sun.

Egon Scharfheber rode his bicycle to the Erdinger Beer depot as he did every morning. As he rode along, he tried to notice what was different, but nothing seemed unusual. The street sweeper was out in front of the grocery, where he often was, pushing a few scraps of paper and some leaves off the sidewalk and into the gutter with his broom. A few women with baskets on their arms were lined up. Some had ration cards in their hands. An old man was walking his dog. The church bell chimed eight. Everything was as it should be.

Egon signed in at the depot. He tried to flirt with Hildegaard at the front desk, but she ignored him. There was nothing unusual about that. Herr Lutz, the dispatcher, wasn't there yet, but the routes for the week were listed on the blackboard. Egon's route had him driving east to Bad Tölz, then to Rosenheim, up to Bad Aibling, then Ebersberg, with stops along the way, then to Munich for a pickup, then out to Passau where he had three deliveries. He would spend a night in Munich and a night in Passau. Munich scared him with all the air raids. But he liked Passau. He knew a girl there. The schedule for the rest of the week seemed pretty routine, too.

Egon was impatient. His truck was loaded. He already had his route. He was ready to go. But Lutz still wasn't there, and he couldn't leave until he signed him out.

'Where the hell is he?' said Egon, half to himself, half to Hildegaard.

'He'll be along,' said Hildegaard.

When Herr Lutz finally showed up, he had another man with him. 'My brother-in-law,' he said. 'Werner Krosius. The wife's brother.'

'I know what brother-in-law means,' said Egon. Lutz was always talking down to him.

'He's going to Passau to start a new job,' said Lutz. 'He'll be riding with you.'

'That's not allowed, is it?' said Egon.

'It's been cleared with Herr Annauer,' said Lutz.

'Do you have it in writing?' said Egon. It had just dawned on him that this might be an umbrella on a sunny day, and he should have something to show the lieutenant. Herr Lutz just looked at him.

The brother-in-law, Werner, turned out to be the perfect travel

partner. He was friendly and knew lots of funny stories, some
of them dirty but none of them dangerous. He even helped Egon
with his deliveries. Egon liked him immediately. Werner had
brought along a few black-market items – he had some women's
stockings, some tinned sardines, and a few other items in his
rucksack.

Egon had brought black bread, cheese, a sausage, a few radishes
for lunch. Werner opened a can of sardines and shared them with
Egon. And they had all the beer they wanted. 'That's one of the
benefits of the job,' said Egon. They ate at a roadside table under
some willow trees not far from Rosenheim.

Werner wondered what were some of the other benefits of
being a beer-truck driver, and Egon told him how every day was
a little different, and you got to travel all over Bavaria. He could
sell a few liters of gas each trip; all the drivers did it, and Herr
Lutz got a little cut.

Werner laughed. 'He acts so innocent, Lutzi does.'

'I'm not supposed to say it, but I'm quasi-SS.' That was out
of the blue and apropos of nothing, but Egon had been dying to
tell.

'Really? That sounds important,' said Werner.

Egon confessed that he was new at it, that he was just getting
the hang of it.

'So what's involved?' said Werner.

'I'm not allowed to say,' said Egon.

'Of course; I understand. Sorry I asked.'

'SS Lieutenant Laumann in Murnau, he wants me to look out
for anything unusual.'

'Unusual? Like what?' said Werner.

'Like someone carrying an umbrella on a sunny day. That's
just an example of the kind of thing.'

'Hmm,' said Werner. 'An umbrella?'

'I don't know. To be honest, Werner, it's not a job I wanted.
I got in a bit of trouble a while back, and Laumann got hold of
my case and kind of made me do this. I'm just not that good at
it. I don't think that way. I'm too trusting of people, and things
seem the way they should be. Know what I mean?'

'Not exactly,' said Werner.

'Well, like today, what happened today that was unusual?

Nothing really. Herr Lutz was a little late and he's usually on time.'

'Well, that was because of me. I wasn't quite ready when he came to pick me up. Come to think of it, my riding along with you, that's unusual, isn't it?'

'Well, it's not normally allowed, but no, Werner, that seems pretty normal to me. It's the kind of thing people do for each other.'

'Well, you're not supposed to have passengers, right? Hey, Egon, why don't you tell your SS lieutenant, what's his name? Laumann?'

'Yeah.'

'Tell Laumann you had a suspicious passenger.'

'Suspicious?' Egon laughed.

'Sure. I don't mind, if it helps you out. It wouldn't bother me.'

'You're a good guy, Werner, but I couldn't do that.' Egon lifted his beer bottle and clinked it against Werner's.

In Munich, Werner knew some girls who were free that night. One of the girls gave them supper, a liver dumpling soup she had just made. They drank beer and laughed and talked until late into the night. Egon's girl let him kiss her but didn't want to go any further. He could have been angry, but he was feeling mellow, so he let it go. Before long, he was asleep on her couch.

The drive to Passau the next day was just as pleasant. Werner knew how to put Egon at ease. He kept trying to help out by suggesting unusual things he noticed that Egon could report. 'The chimney sweep there on the bike could be a saboteur,' he said. 'You can't tell what he looks like underneath all the soot.'

'That's too Hollywood,' said Egon. 'That's what Laumann would say.' Egon told Werner all about SS Lieutenant Klaus Peter Laumann. He was a Prussian. He didn't know Bavarians very well. He was forcing people to inform, and they didn't like it. They were supposed to help him catch an American pilot. There was also a group of traffickers he wanted to catch. 'Be careful with your canned sardines,' said Egon, 'or he'll pull you in.'

'Thanks for the warning,' said Werner. 'I'll be careful.' Egon told Werner about Sepp Krupke.

Werner suggested they keep their eyes open for the pilot. 'Do you know where he was last seen? It would be something, wouldn't it, if you could bring him in?'

Egon said the pilot had been shot down somewhere over Munich. He had recently been seen near Murnau. Egon slowed the truck for a look whenever they saw someone walking alone.

Early in the evening, Egon dropped Werner at his destination in Passau. They shook hands. 'Good luck with the new job,' said Egon. 'Look me up the next time you're in Murnau.'

'I will,' said Werner. 'Maybe we can do a little business.' Whatever that meant.

Egon made his last deliveries of the day. He was in a good mood. He decided to look up the girl he knew. She was at home, and this time she let him have his way.

Plumbing Supplies

Werner Krosius was interviewing for a job as the accountant for Donau Fixtures, a plumbing supply company. The previous accountant had been killed during a bombing raid. There weren't many qualified men around. The owner of the company wondered why Werner wasn't in the army. 'I'm too old,' said Werner. He said he was nearly fifty.

'You don't look it,' said the owner, as though Werner might be up to a trick. Then he sighed and said, 'Oh, well, pretty soon they'll be drafting fifty-year-olds.' The owner gave Werner a little test to see whether he knew anything about accounting. The test was easy for Werner. The owner offered Werner the job and made it sound as though he was doing him a favor. Werner knew the pay should be more, but he accepted the offer anyway.

'Do you have a place to live?' said the owner. 'I can rent you a room in my house.'

'I'm staying with a friend,' said Werner.

'A friend?'

'A guy I know.' Werner said it in a way that let the owner know not to ask any more questions. These days you didn't want to know more than you had to.

Werner Krosius had an accountant's facility with facts and figures and a remarkable memory. He could keep ledgers. But he could also keep long lists – names, dates, numbers – in his head. He could calculate risk instantly and with precision. He could figure profit and loss on the spur of the moment.

Such skills were beyond the needs of Donau Fixtures. But for Werner, the job was a front. Werner was a trader in much more than sardines and nylons. He had started out that way back in the thirties. But he had soon built a network of suppliers and customers, and had expanded his product line into alcohol, meat, tobacco, petrol, kerosene, coal, and other products in short supply.

Then, once the Jews began fleeing and leaving their possessions behind, he had started trading in art and furniture. And nowadays, Werner could provide everything. He could get drugs, medical or otherwise. He had recently begun dealing in weapons and ammunition. There were lots lying around Russia, there for the taking if you could get them. And Werner could. He even had an interest in several prostitution rings. These days, nothing was beyond his reach. He had agents everywhere and several lawyers at the ready.

Any of this activity could have put Werner in front of a firing squad, were it not for his highly placed clients. At the top of the list was *Reichsmarschall* Herman Goering, the commander in chief of the German Air Force and close friend of the Führer. Goering had a serious drug habit, and Werner Krosius had been his principal supplier since the beginning of the war, a lucrative business which by itself would have made him a wealthy man. To show his gratitude, he showed up one day at Goering's castle in Mauterndorf, Austria, with a package under his arm. He stood by as Goering cut the string and pulled the paper away. Goering was an avaricious art collector, and his mouth fell open when he saw the painting, a small portrait by Rembrandt of his wife Saskia. 'Herr Krosius, you astonish me,' he said,

'A gift, *Herr Reichsmarschall*,' said Krosius.

'Where did you get it?' said Goering.

Krosius just smiled.

As a kind of insurance, Werner traded in information as well. And he had customers on all sides. What he had learned from Egon Scharfheber about SS Lieutenant Laumann and his hunt for the American pilot and the traffickers could be of value to the underground as well as to certain Nazi officials. No one especially liked someone who traded in information, but everyone needed him.

Krosius understood that sooner or later Germany would lose the war. You didn't have to be an accountant to do the math. German airplanes were being destroyed in the air and on the ground faster than they could be replaced. Tanks and ships were being destroyed just as rapidly. The Russian countryside was strewn with the rotting corpses of German soldiers, and the Soviet army was advancing steadily on Germany. Italy had surrendered to the Allies. And a great force was assembling in England for a massive invasion.

Werner had calculated that Passau on the German, Austrian, and Czech borders was suitably out of the way and would provide the kind of regulatory complexity that would serve his purposes well, and – when the time came – would allow him to disappear.

Werner spent an hour or so each morning going over the ledgers at Donau Fixtures. His predecessor had been careless and lazy, and Werner quickly brought the books into correct compliance. After that, it was simply a matter of keeping up with the small payroll, the invoices, managing inventory – which for a man of Werner's particular skills was child's play. The rest of the day he could tend to his own business.

Because of his other skills, Werner was able to acquire certain plumbing fixtures and supplies that, before he arrived, had been unavailable. The steel, zinc, and lead used in the manufacture of these supplies were military necessities and were embargoed for non-military uses. For three years, Donau Fixtures had been relying on inventory. And then, once those shelves had emptied, they had been repurposing old fixtures and improvising with other inferior ones. Until Werner arrived, that is.

The owner held up a shiny new steel fitting and gazed at it as though he were witnessing a miracle. 'Where the devil did you find this?' he said to Werner.

Werner didn't answer. He knew the owner – like all his customers – didn't really want to know.

The Seduction

It was Friday evening. Egon Scharfheber had made a late delivery at the Gasthof Klemmer in Rosenheim. Herr Klemmer offered him supper for his trouble – a mushroom omelet with real eggs and the year's first asparagus. After dinner, Egon had drunk a little too much. He had dozed off in a chair by the fire.

Liesl, the hotel maid, had stayed late to clean up the banquet room after a birthday celebration. There had been singing, a cake with candles, enough sparkling wine so that everyone got a glass, and even some puff pastries with a tiny dab of chicken liver pâté.

Liesl sat at the bar having her supper. It was nearly ten o'clock. Supper and one beer every evening after work was part of her wages. Some days it was the only meal she got.

Egon woke from his nap. He stretched and yawned loudly. He struggled to his feet and hitched up his pants. Then he noticed Liesl at the bar. She was plump in the right places, had small, twinkly eyes, a pushed-up nose, pink cheeks, red lips, and blond hair. A double chin and a few wrinkles, but so what? *Why not give it a try?* thought Egon.

'Fräulein,' he said, 'a nightcap?'

'No, thank you.'

Egon, still a little drunk, figured she was playing hard to get. 'Come on, Fräulein, we're two working people, you and I, birds of a feather. How about it, sweetheart? Just one drink.'

Herr Klemmer knew Liesl, and he knew Egon. He thought he knew how this was going to turn out.

'No, thanks.'

'Fräulein,' said Egon. 'You don't know me. But I could tell you some things.' He had been refining his 'quasi-SS' story. 'Let me tell you, the things one sees, when he does his duty for the fatherland . . .' He let the unfinished phrase hang in the air.

Liesl looked at Egon with something resembling curiosity. 'All right,' she said. 'One drink. Cognac.'

'And one for me,' said Egon, with a wink at Herr Klemmer.

They took their glasses and sat by the fire. Egon spun out his tale of intrigue and daring in a low voice, embellishing it extravagantly and not skimping on the essential facts either. He had reported a local schoolteacher who was part of the underground. 'I can tell you, Fräulein, this caused dear old Laumann to sit up and take notice. He wrote it all down in his notebook. "Scharfheber," he said, "I want you to follow up on this schoolteacher fellow. Find out who he is, his name, address, et cetera. Then I want you to follow him wherever he goes."'

The truth was, of course, otherwise. On hearing about the so-called underground schoolteacher, Laumann had turned red in the face, jumped out of his chair, dived across his desk, and grabbed Egon by the lapels. 'Damn you to hell, Scharfheber, are you a complete idiot? I need names! Names! Facts! You bring me rumors without meaning. Sergeant!' he screamed. 'Come in here and take this pig away.'

'Wait, *Herr Leutnant*. Wait! I have a name. I have a name. *Of course* I have a name.' He said the first name that came to mind. 'Krosius. Werner Krosius. The brother-in-law of Herr Lutz, my dispatcher. A big-time black marketeer in Passau. I drove him to Passau three days ago. I dropped him at the corner of Kubin and Eichholzstraße. I brought you this information as soon as I could.'

Laumann sat down. He sent the sergeant away and wrote everything down. He asked questions about Krosius, and for once Egon had the answers. 'Finally, Scharfheber. It's about damn time you showed up with something useful.'

Liesl was unimpressed by Egon's story. She tossed back the last sip of her cognac and said, 'I have to go.'

'How about one more, Fräulein.'

'Another time,' she said. She stood up, slipped into her coat, and left, rolling her eyes at Herr Klemmer as she went.

The Alm on the Nagelkopf

C harlie had been standing in the shadows studying the Saturday market in Niederhausen. He turned, and he and the town policeman recognized one another in the same moment. Charlie dashed around a corner, ran through the crowded square, and came out the other side. He ducked into a small wood at the edge of town. The policeman rushed into the square, but got caught in the crowd, and Charlie had disappeared.

'Can I help you?' said a man.

Charlie spun around, ready to run again. But the man raised his hands and said in English, 'I know who you are. I can help you.'

'You know who I am?'

Charlie must have sounded disappointed because the man smiled and said, 'I mean, I know you're in trouble. I can help. Come with me.' Charlie hesitated only a moment, then followed him.

'Are you English?'

'American,' said Charlie.

'Ah,' said the man. 'So you must be the one they're looking for. Before just now, I mean,' said the man, nodding in the direction of the market. 'When pilots are shot down, they're usually caught right away. When they aren't caught right away, there's usually an all-out manhunt, and the word gets around.'

The man – he said his name was Andreas – took Charlie to his home. He gave him a warm meal. After dark, they walked to the Zoellners' farm where Helga Zoellner fed him again.

Early the next morning, Jürgen Zoellner walked Charlie up to the *Alm* – his summer pasture. It was a long, steep climb along logging roads, then beside a tumbling mountain stream, and through an enormous forest of gigantic fir trees. Jürgen didn't speak English, so they walked in silence. After two hours, they reached the hut above the *Alm*. They drank water from the pump and rested on the porch. Jürgen unlocked the cabin and opened the shutters. He signaled that Charlie shouldn't make a fire. He pointed to his eyes and then toward the valley to indicate that the smoke would be seen from below.

'*Keine Feuer*,' Charlie said. Or was it *kein Feuer*? He couldn't remember.

'*Kein Feuer*,' said Jürgen. He smiled for the first time.

'*Ich verstehe*,' said Charlie, smiling back.

Jürgen made sure there were blankets for the cot, then headed back down the mountain.

There was no moon that night. There was no wind, and it was cold. The sky was lit by a million stars. Charlie was glad he still had the sheepskin.

He woke up early the next morning. He sat at the edge of the wooden porch warmed by the rising sun, his feet resting on the boulder that served as a step. He cut a hunk of cheese from the yellow wedge beside him. He cut a slice of onion. He put them both on a thick slab of black bread and took a big bite. He had to tear at the crust with his teeth. It was thick, chewy, and delicious. He took a big drink of apple cider.

From his vantage in front of the hut, Charlie saw the world spread in front of him: first the pasture, rich, green, sprinkled with wildflowers, then the evergreen forest below, then the tree-tops, the nearby stony peaks above, and beyond them the fields and forests stretching into the blue haze to the north.

Charlie had wandered across a large corner of Bavaria. And although he was a hunted man, he had convinced himself he would be fine, that he would reach France, England, and eventually Ohio. When you're only twenty-three, you tend to think that way. But now he thought of what Andreas had said. There was an all-out manhunt. If he fell into the hands of the SS, they would find out quickly enough that he had been in intelligence, if they didn't already know. They would want to know about the coming invasion, and while Charlie's intelligence work had to do with targeting bombing runs, interpreting aerial photos, that sort of thing, they would be convinced that he knew about the invasion. And they would do whatever they had to do to get it out of him.

The Tangled Web

A letter had reached Willi from someone known to him only by his or her code name, Daisy.

Daisy had learned that a schoolteacher in the Murnau area was suspected by the SS of belonging to the underground. Daisy didn't know if the SS knew who the schoolteacher was or whether there even was such a schoolteacher. But if there was, he should be warned and probably withdrawn from action.

Daisy also wrote that a black marketeer in Passau named Werner Krosius was also known to the SS. Daisy knew this thanks to a source and SS informant named Egon Scharfheber.

Daisy did not know whether Krosius could be helpful or dangerous to their cause but thought he might be a source of information. Finally, Daisy warned that Egon Scharfheber was a fool and a braggart. But there was little doubt he was informing SS Lieutenant Klaus Peter Laumann and would know something about SS activity in the area.

After reading the letter, Willi decided he should go to Murnau.

'You're jeopardizing security, you're violating your own rules,' said Lola. 'You're acting like you're solving a crime.'

'I'm trying to solve a crime before it happens,' he said. 'I'm trying to prevent a crime. It's pretty much the same thing.' A downed American pilot, whose approximate whereabouts were known to the police and the SS, was now at the Zoellners' *Alm*. 'I need to be sure that when the moment comes to get him over the border, I have the whole picture – obstacles, pitfalls, everything. It all has to go just right.'

Willi called Pierre's number. The same woman always answered. Willi mentioned a place and time. Willi bicycled to where Pierre was waiting with a car.

Pierre had refused a flower name. 'I am just Pierre,' he said. 'How is that less secure than Sunflower or Lily?' He had a point. Nobody knew anything about Pierre, not even his last name.

They knew he had an accent that sounded vaguely French. They knew he was a gifted driver. That was all.

Pierre liked for Willi to ride in the back seat. 'Just in case,' said Pierre. Whatever that meant. They drove fast on small back roads. Pierre didn't need a map.

'Have you always driven?' said Willi.

'Since I was six,' said Pierre. He might have been joking. You couldn't tell.

They reached Murnau in an hour. 'There is the SS,' said Pierre, pointing to a yellow building draped in swastika flags as they sped past.

It was fifteen more minutes to the green house. Pierre parked the car out of sight. He walked down to the lake and smoked while Willi talked with Fedor.

'The SS knows there's a schoolteacher in the underground. And they may know more than that,' said Willi. 'They may know it's you.'

'I understand,' said Fedor, but he didn't really. He wanted to be involved in every rescue operation.

Willi wanted Fedor to step back, but he didn't want to force the issue. If he pushed too hard, Fedor would get his back up, and then there would be no stopping him from going when it came time to move the American. 'Fair enough,' said Willi. 'Tell me what you know about the SS lieutenant in Murnau, named Laumann.'

'Klaus Peter Laumann,' said Fedor. 'A sour but not unintelligent man. He doesn't like being stationed here. He's made that plain.'

'You know him, then?'

'Met him. At a meeting he called to get acquainted with "community elders" after he arrived. I was one of twenty-five or thirty. He wouldn't remember me.'

Willi let it drop. 'What about a man named Krosius, black marketeer, just moved to Passau?'

'Werner Krosius. I've heard of him. He has a pretty substantial operation from what I understand. I didn't know he'd gone to Passau.'

'What's he like, Fedor?'

'He's smart, likable, smooth, and thoroughly corrupt, from what I hear. He must have friends in high places.'

'What makes you say that?'

'Everybody knows about him, and yet nothing ever happens to him. If he weren't protected, he'd be in Dachau by now.'

When Werner Krosius had suggested to Egon that he should feel free to turn him in to Laumann, he knew he was safe. At the same time, he wanted to get to know the SS lieutenant in charge in Murnau, so being turned in was one way to bring it about. When Werner was finally visited by an SS contingent sent to arrest him, he produced a letter from SS Lieutenant General Ludvig von Hoepner, chief of SS operations in the southern sector. The chief arresting sergeant read the letter, handed it back to Werner, and saluted. Werner assured the sergeant that he had every intention of complying with Lieutenant Laumann's 'request' and promised to be at his office bright and early the next morning. And so he was. For an hour, he and Laumann danced around one another. Laumann wanted information about the Flower Gang. Werner said he would provide him with information as he got it. In exchange, he wanted freedom of movement and operation in the Murnau sector. They promised each other complete cooperation, neither one feeling at all bound by his promise.

One morning, Jürgen and the dog came up the mountain accompanied by two men. One was smallish and thin, wearing a heavy tweed jacket and a plaid necktie, and looking more like a schoolmaster than a member of the underground. Fedor Blaskowitz explained that it was better if Charlie didn't know his name. He could think of him as Geranium. 'Herr Geranium, if you like,' he said, laughing.

The other man, Willi Geismeier, was tall and slender and exuded patience. His clothes were a little shabby: a heavy wool sweater under a baggy jacket, baggy trousers, and heavy walking shoes. He had a relaxed easiness about him, especially alongside the jumpy Geranium. He had a nice face, but the kind you might forget the moment he was out of sight. 'I'm Dandelion,' he said with a slight smile.

Geranium proceeded to do most of the talking, but Charlie had the sense that Dandelion was in charge. Geranium explained that the SS hunt for Charlie had intensified since he had run from the policeman in Niederhausen. They were doing searches and interrogations all over town. 'It should die down in a few days, if you lie low. Eventually, they'll assume you've moved on.'

Charlie didn't like hearing he was expected to stay put. He had been doing all right on his own, he said. He wondered what Geranium meant by a few days. Fedor shrugged. He didn't know, he said. Few pilots had managed to avoid being caught as long as Charlie had. But the longer you were at large, the more the circle tightened and the more likely you were to be caught.

'I did all right on my own,' said Charlie again.

'You didn't,' said Dandelion. 'Otherwise, Murnau wouldn't be full of SS looking for you. And you won't. And if you tried to go on your own, you would jeopardize our operation as well. So you have to be patient.'

Charlie was about to argue, but something in Dandelion's face stopped him. 'Who's going to go with me?'

'That hasn't been decided yet,' said Dandelion.

'Probably a different flower,' said Geranium, laughing harder than his joke deserved.

Geranium asked Charlie what else he needed for the trip and whether he was feeling strong.

Charlie said he was feeling strong. He exercised every day. He said he would like a razor and shaving soap if it wasn't too much trouble.

Geranium said it wouldn't be any trouble at all.

Something to read, maybe, said Charlie.

'An excellent idea,' said Geranium.

'In English,' said Charlie.

Willi asked Charlie whether he had a .45 or any other weapon. Charlie said he didn't. Pilots were advised to leave their sidearms at home. If you were captured in civilian clothes with a weapon, that made you a terrorist or a spy and not a prisoner of war. That meant Dachau or worse, instead of a POW camp.

'What was your branch before you flew?' said Dandelion.

'Intelligence,' said Charlie. 'Why?'

'What sort of intelligence exactly?'

'Targeting and interpretation,' said Charlie. 'Why are you asking?'

'If you're caught by the SS, that's what they'll focus on,' said Dandelion.

'They won't know.'

'They *will* know. By now, they know more about you than you can imagine.'

'I'd be a prisoner of war,' said Charlie.

'That doesn't matter to them,' said Dandelion. 'What do you know about the invasion?' he said.

'Nothing,' said Charlie.

'Listen,' said Dandelion. 'Nothing is what the German High Command knows. They don't know the when or the where, the how or the who. What do *you* know?'

Charlie gave Willi a long, hard look. Charlie knew the plan was for June fifth, sixth, or seventh on the beaches of Normandy. He knew about Operation Fortitude, designed to trick the Germans into thinking it would be further up the coast. He had seen the dummy tanks and landing crafts built by the thousands in Kent to make it look as if the invasion would come across the channel at Calais. 'I know nothing,' said Charlie again.

'I don't believe you, and they won't either,' said Dandelion. 'I don't want to know, so it doesn't matter to me. But you need to be ready to give them something. Because if it comes to that, they won't let up until you do.'

Herr Schacht

Werner Krosius had lunch most days at the Gasthaus Steinpilz not far from his office at Donau Fixtures. He sat at a table by the kitchen. It was his regular table, where he could meet clients and suppliers. It was separate from the six other tables, and at the same time he could see who came and went.

Werner had never seen Willi before, but there was something about him that caught his eye. The way he sat down at the table by the door as though it were his. That he sat there at all, not reluctant to be seen, his apparent indifference to others, including Werner, set him apart. Werner wondered whether he might be Gestapo. He decided he had better find out.

Willi sipped his potato soup. It needed salt, so he signaled the waiter who brought salt.

'Do you know that man?' Werner asked the waiter, gesturing with his head in Willi's direction.

The waiter looked. 'No,' he said.

'Seen him before?'

'I don't think so,' said the waiter.

Willi finished his soup. He asked for the check, paid for the soup, two rolls, and a small beer. 'The soup was delicious,' he said and smiled.

'*Danke, mein Herr*,' said the waiter and gave Willi his change.

As Willi rose to leave, Werner came up to him. 'It's Herr Schacht, isn't it?' he said and held out his hand.

'Yes,' said Willi, offering his own hand. 'It's Herr Schacht.'

This surprised Werner. He had expected Willi to deny being Herr Schacht, since Werner had made it up. He had gone fishing and had been caught himself.

Krosius tried again. 'I'm Werner Krosius,' he said. 'I'm sure we've met.'

'I'm pretty sure we haven't, Herr Krosius,' said Willi, slipping into his jacket.

'Haven't we had business dealings?' said Werner.

'No. I don't think so,' said Willi. 'I don't trade in the black market.'

Two nearby tables were occupied. Werner didn't know whether they had heard, but both tables went quiet. He smiled and nodded in their direction, and they looked away.

Willi left the restaurant, and Werner followed. Werner suggested they should talk further. Willi didn't know what they had to talk about, but he had no objection. He meant to take a walk along the River Inn, and Krosius was welcome to join him.

'You're not from Passau, are you?' said Werner, dropping the pretense that they knew each other.

'No,' said Willi. 'I'm not. Are you?'

'No. I moved here recently.'

'I see,' said Willi.

'In my business . . .'

'Your business?' said Willi.

'I call it trading.'

'Aha,' said Willi.

'It's not just goods, you know. It's also services,' said Werner. 'Of all kinds. In my business,' he began again, 'Passau is a good place to be. And what business are you in, Herr Schacht?'

Willi ignored Werner's question. 'I don't get to Passau often. I like it here, though. What exactly do you trade in?'

'Whatever interests you, Herr . . .?'

'Schacht,' said Willi.

'Well, Herr Schacht, I can get pretty much anything. At the moment, I'm involved in currency trading. And sex, of course. Sex is always a good trade. It never goes out of style. What interests you?'

Willi laughed. 'Your openness is . . . amazing. You don't seem at all worried about telling a complete stranger what you're up to.'

'Well, Herr Schacht, you're not a complete stranger, are you? I know something about you. I mean, you're willing to consort with a black marketeer, even if it's only for a walk and a talk. And you're a man with your own secrets; that's pretty obvious. I thought you were Gestapo at first, but now I suspect you're on the other side.'

'Is that so?' said Willi.

'There's a gang, for instance,' said Krosius. 'They're quite notorious. You must have heard of them. They use the names of flowers as their *noms de guerre*. It's a silly affectation, don't you think? Still, they seem to be a particular thorn in the side of the Gestapo. Are you political, Herr Schacht?'

'Political? No,' said Willi.

'Good. Neither am I. I work all sides. What do you trade in, Herr Schacht?'

'I don't trade in anything, Herr Krosius.'

Werner suddenly stopped walking and looked hard at Willi. 'You're looking for information, aren't you?'

'Information? Sure, why not? For instance, how do you think the war is going, Herr Krosius?' said Willi.

Krosius laughed. 'Now, there is a question that could get us both in a lot of trouble. You for asking, and me for answering.' Werner hesitated only a moment. 'The war is lost, Herr Schacht. Only, Hitler doesn't know it, or rather doesn't *want* to know it. The Russians are closing in from the east. There will be a great Allied invasion in the west – everyone knows that – and that will be the end. The word I have is that the invasion will be at Calais, probably in the next few weeks. That's what the general staff believes and what they're preparing for.'

'Are you this frank with your Nazi patrons, Herr Krosius, with Lieutenant Laumann and the others?' said Willi.

'About the war? Of course not. I depend on their self-delusion. Although Laumann is no patron. He is a customer. Like you, Herr Schacht.'

Willi smiled. 'And will you tell him about me, Herr Krosius?'

Werner thought for a moment. 'That depends. If it is helpful for me to do so, I might. I can offer you something about Laumann, though – something you might find useful.'

'And what is your price?' said Willi.

'Gratis, Herr Schacht. Consider it a gift. I like to be helpful when I can. Laumann is determined to get his hands on a missing American fighter pilot, a Captain Charles Herder, an intelligence officer, and then to use him to catch the underground organization, the Flower Gang, that's protecting him.'

'And why would that interest me?' said Willi.

'No particular reason,' said Krosius and smiled.

After a while, the men parted company. Willi walked to where he was to meet Pierre. 'Don't drive too fast, Pierre,' he said. After a while, he said, 'Are we being followed?'

'I think so,' said Pierre. 'Shall I lose him?'

'No,' said Willi. 'Don't lose him.'

Men

Krosius worried Willi. An unprincipled opportunist, playing both sides, was in some ways the most dangerous enemy of all. However, when Lola asked Willi about his trip, all he said at first was that it had been helpful. He didn't tell her about the American pilot or about Krosius.

After Willi had spent time in Dachau, he and Lola had agreed that the less information they had about each other, the safer it was for them both. When she left on an assignment, she would say only, 'I'm going out.'

'All right,' he said. That was all. Never 'Be careful,' nothing to indicate he was worried. Certainly never 'Come back safely' or 'I love you.' Those were words you spoke in safer times. Now, 'I love you' would be a distraction. It could lead to unsafe thoughts and dangerous behavior.

Their love for one another had moved underground, like the rest of their lives. They expressed their affection and caring in as few words as possible. They made love rarely and then with frightening intensity, which they always worried about afterwards. In the world where he was Dandelion and she was Tulip, any and every connection was dangerous, and loving someone was especially dangerous. And yet Krosius had planted doubts in his mind that needed sorting out.

'I'm a little worried about Fedor,' said Willi. Lola filled Willi's bowl and then her own with lentil soup. Their kitchen window looked out to the west where the sun was just setting. The towering clouds had turned red. 'The SS may be on to him. But, dammit, he's determined to take the pilot to the border. Fedor knows the way, the safe houses, all of it. But he's unfamiliar with the border. And there's always the . . . unpredictable element. Somebody has to go with them. Maybe I should go.'

Lola sliced bread. She put pickles and sausage on a plate and set it between them. She opened a bottle of beer and put it and two glasses on the table. The entire room had turned red from the sunset. She sat down, and they looked out at the clouds. 'No,' she said finally, 'it can't be you.'

'I know Fedor, and he knows me,' said Willi. 'That's an advantage.'

'Not much of one,' said Lola. 'And neither of you knows the border. That's a big disadvantage. The other problem is that, whether you like it or not, you're the center that holds things together. If you're caught, then the whole thing goes up in flames.'

'I can't ask others to take risks I'm not willing to take.'

'Stop that, Willi.'

'Stop what?' he said.

'Stop being such a man,' said Lola. It was not meant as a compliment. 'You think it's about you, and not about what makes the most sense.'

'Then you tell me: what makes the most sense?' he said.

'Sending someone who knows the border makes sense. The SS will be all over the border. Send someone who knows the area, where a crossing is possible.'

Willi named a couple of prospects: a mountaineer in Ravensburg came to mind; a student in Freiburg was another.

'Elke Oldenburg,' said Lola. 'Clover.'

'Really? Why?'

'Don't you remember she used to live there, in Konstanz?'

Willi had forgotten. 'She's very young,' he said.

'She's twenty-two or three. How old is your pilot?'

Willi raised more objections, and one by one Lola knocked them down.

That was how Elke found herself beside Willi in the back seat of a car driven by Pierre and speeding toward the green house on the Riegsee. They had to pull over once when she got sick. 'Sorry,' she said. 'I haven't ridden in a car for a long time.'

Fedor had only seen a few black Germans and had never met one. He was startled when she got out of the car. She pulled her rucksack from the trunk and offered Fedor her hand. 'Clover,' she said. Fedor smiled, thinking to himself, no matter what her real name was, Clover suited her better.

Pierre drove them to the trail that led to the *Alm*. Willi, Fedor, and Elke made the hike up in just under two hours. Charlie had been out walking above the *Alm* and saw them from a distance. He walked down to meet them.

Willi and Fedor shook hands with Charlie. Willi introduced Elke as Clover. 'When the time comes, Clover and Geranium will get you to the border.'

Charlie looked Elke up and down. He looked back and forth from Willi to Fedor and back again. 'A colored girl? Are you kidding?'

Neither Willi nor Fedor could quite believe what they had just heard.

'What did you say?' said Willi.

Charlie Herder had grown up in the Price Hill section of Cincinnati, the eldest of five children. His father Russell had come up from Corbin, Kentucky, looking for work. His mother Alma had grown up on a farm in Winchester, Kentucky.

Russell and Alma believed, like all their kin and much of America, in what they called good Christian values: fear of God, and that the white race was God's greatest creation. They were sure they were superior in every way to blacks, Jews, and all the other 'races.' Russell the father was an active member of the Ku Klux Klan, an organization with millions of members at that time. He marched with them through the streets of Cincinnati, in defense of his white heritage and against blacks voting or gaining any other measure of justice and equality.

Charlie the son believed in all this just as fervently as his father and mother did. But being a modern Christian man, with what he took to be a deep sense of humility and moderation, despite his hatred for blacks, he never used the word 'nigger.' That small concession was how he convinced himself that his beliefs were based on facts and not on prejudice. Using that word would have shown a bias he could never admit to. He was as certain as any man can be that his racial hatred was not prejudice or bigotry but was based on established facts that anyone with good sense could readily observe.

Willi stared at Charlie, while Fedor and Elke turned away.

Finally, Charlie said, 'A colored girl? I'd rather make the trip on my own.'

'You don't have that choice,' said Willi.

'What do you mean?' said Charlie, getting angry.

'Listen to me, Captain Herder,' said Willi. 'Geranium and Clover are going to take you to the border when the time comes. If you do anything to interfere with them, or if you do anything to endanger them, we'll call them off and, I promise you, the SS will have you in a matter of hours.'

'What? You mean you'd turn me in?' said Charlie.

'No, I wouldn't turn you in,' said Willi. 'I wouldn't have to. The Gestapo knows who you are by now. They have a pretty good idea where you are. They'd catch you like that.' He snapped his fingers right in front of Charlie's face.

Waiting

Charlie had gone back inside the hut. It was after seven in the evening. The sun was low in the sky, the temperature was dropping. For Willi, Fedor, and Elke to get back down the mountain before dark, they'd have to leave soon.

'Does this change our plan?' said Fedor.

'I don't think so,' said Willi. 'He stays here until the invasion. Tomorrow or however long it takes. We need the distraction of the invasion to make this work.' He turned to Elke. 'How are you?'

'What do you mean?' she said. 'Do you think that shit was a shock for me? I've dealt with people like that all my life. My own mother wasn't much better. Our plan's a good one.'

'OK. Let's go ahead,' said Willi. 'I suggest one change, though: that you stay here with him until it's time to go.'

Elke studied Willi for a long moment.

'It's up to you,' said Willi.

'I don't get it,' said Fedor. 'Why subject her to all that hate and abuse?'

'You're right,' said Willi. 'That's unfair. But we're also subjecting him to Clover's competence. What do you think, Clover?' Elke gave Willi another long look. Then she laughed.

Charlie thought they must have left when he heard a knock at the door. He opened it to see the colored girl standing there, her rucksack hanging on her arm as if she meant to stay. The two men were already at the bottom of the pasture getting close to the trees. He watched as they disappeared into the forest.

When Charlie didn't move, Elke stepped around him and into the hut. The cot where Charlie had been sleeping was in one corner. She carried her rucksack to the opposite corner. She pulled cushions from two chairs and made a bed on the floor. She took out some food she had brought – some sausage, rye bread, and a big slab of apple strudel wrapped in waxed paper. She held out the food in Charlie's direction. He turned away.

Charlie tried to read, but his mind wouldn't let him. The colored girl lay wrapped in her coat on the cushions. She was sleeping. He could hear her long, deep breaths. Something about her calm made him even angrier. He lay down on the cot and tossed about, first one way, then the other. For a long time, he couldn't sleep, but eventually he did.

Elke woke up as the dim first light of morning was seeping through the window. Charlie had packed up his belongings during the night. His rucksack stood by the door. He had lit the candle. His map was spread out on the cot, and he was studying it. He noticed her looking at him. 'I'm leaving,' he said.

She looked at him and shrugged.

'Christ!' he said. 'She doesn't even speak English. *Ich . . . gehe! . . . Allein!*'

Clover came over and looked at the map. She pointed to a spot on the map and then pointed at Charlie and herself.

'Christ, *Missy,* I know where we are. And I'm going here.' He jabbed his finger at the French border, then jabbed it again for emphasis.

She put her finger on the map and said, '*SS Kommando hier.*' She slid her finger a little to the west. '*Polizei hier,*' she said. She moved her finger again. '*Mehr Polizei.*' And again. '*Mehr Polizei.*' And again. '*SS Kommando.*' And again. '*Luftwaffe.*' And again. '*Gestapo.*'

She moved her finger once more before he tore the map away. 'OK, OK,' he said. 'I get it!'

Charlie handed her a pencil. 'Mark them.'

She just looked at him.

'I said mark them, goddammit!'

Elke laid the pencil down and walked away.

Charlie had never had a real conversation with a black man or woman. When he had to speak to one, he tried to be polite, but not necessarily respectful. Their worlds were separate; their lives did not intersect. They were inferior to him.

But now this affront – this was something he found intolerable. He had never before been treated with such disrespect by a black man or woman. She wouldn't have dared back home. This was what happened when you started giving blacks rights and privileges. They always took advantage, they always pushed things too far. You needed to keep the lines distinct, clear, or this is what happened.

He thought allowing American blacks to vote was a big mistake. They were too ignorant to vote responsibly. They could serve in the army, which Charlie was also against. As far as he was concerned, they didn't have courage and couldn't follow orders. And now there were colored pilots, for Christ's sake. What was the army thinking? Flying a plane was complicated. You needed to make split-second decisions. And once they got in trouble, they would cut and run, like the colored always did. They were natural-born cowards.

OK, yes. He needed help to get to the border. But Christ almighty! A fucking colored girl? It was just a fucking insult! These fucking Krauts just wanted to put him in his place. And their fucking flower names! What the fuck was that about? It was like they were playing a fucking game.

Charlie had worked himself into a rage. He held the map in his clenched fists, pretending to study it. But it was all he could do to contain his fury and confusion. As he swung around to confront Elke yet again, he knocked the candle over, catching the map on fire. He dropped it on to the floor and stamped it out with his feet.

When he looked up, she was watching him. Before he could speak, she did. '*Hauptmann Herder, hören Sie mich gut zu.*' Then in English, 'You listen to me, Captain.' *Jesus*, thought Charlie, *so she does speak English. Then why didn't she . . .? Just like a damn . . .!* He wouldn't say the word, but he thought it.

'You are a stranger in Germany, Captain,' she said. 'You do not know much German. You do not know the country. You do not know the people. You do not know where the enemy is waiting for you or even what the enemy looks like. You do not know anything. But you imagine you know everything.

'Geranium and I will be taking you across the border. We will do our best to get you there safely, but we need you to cooperate. You may be a captain in the US army. But here, I am in charge. Do you understand me?'

Charlie was so mad he could hardly think. It was true he didn't know anything about Germany or any of the people trying to help him. But what kind of fly-by-night operation put a colored girl in charge? She had goaded him and made him look foolish.

Yet somewhere behind his fury and unhappiness, in a back corner of his brain, he understood that he had better listen to the girl they called Clover, at least for the time being. Even if she was impudent. Even if she was colored.

He hated having to think this way. His sense of superiority over black people was not something he usually even thought about. It was so deeply and thoroughly embedded in his character, such an integral part of who he was, that it seemed genetic, like his pale skin itself. And his current situation didn't change any of that.

His white skin and Clover's black skin – not the situation – should have determined his superiority and her inferiority. That was how things were supposed to be.

OK, maybe he had been a little bit wrong about her. She spoke better English than he spoke German. She seemed to know what she was talking about. It looked like he didn't have any other choice. But she was still a colored girl. The flower boys were in charge, and there was nothing he could do about that either.

For some reason, the black fighter pilots came to mind again. He had recently heard about the Red Tails, this squadron of black fighter pilots escorting bombers out of North Africa and Italy. According to what he had heard, more than once even, they were skillful and effective. They had lost fewer bombers, they had destroyed more enemy aircraft in the air and on the ground, and they had been shot down fewer times and suffered fewer casualties than the white squadrons. And yet that just couldn't be. They just *had* to be bad pilots because they were *colored*.

Because Charlie believed in and lived by a wrong and evil principle, and because commitment to that principle was both stupid and unjust, his mind was all the more unchangeable. That is the way we humans are: the dumber our beliefs, the more desperately we cling to them. His belief caused him to see things as he wanted them to be, and not as they were. But what if the Red Tails *were* better pilots than the white pilots? What if they were better pilots than Charlie was?

No, no! They couldn't be! Charlie was an excellent pilot. Getting shot down was just tough luck, a fluke. It proved nothing.

Charlie had dismissed the Red Tails when he first heard of their exploits, and he was doing it again, against all reason or purpose, against everything he had heard and *knew* was probably true. But dismissing them came naturally, like breathing. It was what happened automatically when he strayed into unreasonable territory. He had persisted, and persisted still, in disparaging the black pilots for no reason other than because he had always done so. It was the central fact of his existence, and there was no reason to change now. Full stop. End of story. But you had the Red Tails, and *now* you had the colored girl, Clover, and . . .

Charlie had just admitted the fatal question into his mind: how could he think of himself as a reasonable and intelligent man and yet continue to reject things he *saw* were true, he *knew* were true? But they weren't true! His mind was playing tricks on him. His mother would have said it was the devil at work, undermining his heritage, his beliefs, his essence. All the things he thought about the colored, the pilots, the colored girl were the *real* reality. 'Always be true, Charlie,' his mother said.

'I will, Mamma,' he said.

Except now it was as if Charlie had somehow driven at high speed on to a circular racetrack. He was driving in circles again and again when he had meant to be going in a straight line. He was chasing his thoughts around and around, always arriving back at the same spot, whizzing past the same inescapable conviction that things were as he wanted them to be, as he was sure they were, then passing again the same conclusion that, no, things must be as they actually were.

All of this was, of course, too much to take in or even acknowledge right away. But at least Charlie understood his situation well enough in this moment to be able to respond to Clover's admonition, 'I am in charge; do you understand?' by saying, 'Yes, I understand.' He said it grudgingly, even contemptuously. He admitted nothing, offered no respect, committed to nothing. 'I understand' meant nothing more than the words implied: he understood the words she had spoken. He was content to leave it like that until he could sort things out.

Information

S S Lieutenant Laumann's efforts to build a network of informants had borne fruit. He had gone over the report from the Niederhausen police detailing the sighting of the American pilot. The policeman had lost him in the crowded market square. But a witness had come forward who had seen a man duck into the woods after the pilot. The witness was not certain but thought he recognized the man as Andreas Neurath, a local schoolteacher. Laumann concluded that Neurath might be the teacher rumored to be part of the underground, so he was having him watched.

From Uwe Pfeiffer, the town grocer, came a report that Helga Zoellner, the farmer's wife, had recently changed her shopping habits and was now buying more food than had previously been her practice. The grocer was one of those overenthusiastic people who, once he learned people were betraying the Führer, reported a thousand infractions – real and imagined – committed by his neighbors, reports intended mainly to prove his own virtue.

Frau Zoellner explained to two of Laumann's SS men that the extra provisions were all within her rationed allowance and amounted to some extra sugar, flour, a few other things. And that from those things she had made a cake and a small banquet for herself, her husband, her sister, and her sister's husband to commemorate the death of their son who had died in Russia for the Fatherland. Laumann's SS men seemed satisfied she was telling the truth. Still, they searched the premises. The lieutenant would have come down on them hard if they hadn't.

They had never been inside a Bavarian farmhouse. No one in Berlin lived like this. The house and barn were one enormous structure with carved and painted timbers supporting a massive stone roof. There were painted balconies in front of every window. The doors, shutters, and window frames were also carved and gaily painted in red, yellow, and green. There were huge painted armoires where you could hide a man and all his belongings.

There were sleeping alcoves tucked into the walls, covered with great quilts, and closed off by heavy curtains. Even the cow barn was decorated with paintings and carvings on the doors and timbers.

They waded gingerly through the cows and searched the hay barn and the milking shed by the pasture as well. Laumann read through the Zoellner report twice. Something was missing. Then he remembered Bavarian farmers took their cows to the mountains for the summer.

'Where were the cows?' he asked the two Berliners.

'In the pasture,' said one of the men.

'Which pasture? Up or down?' said Laumann.

The men were puzzled. Laumann explained about the *Alm*.

'They were just outside the village. The winter pasture, I guess.'

'Did she say anything about the summer pasture?' said Laumann.

'No,' said the Berliners.

'Go find out why,' said Laumann.

In the meantime, Laumann had seen Werner Krosius. Krosius said he needed a favor. Some of his supply chains had been disrupted by the SS, and in exchange for relaxation of the controls, he offered information he thought Laumann would find useful.

Laumann wanted to hear the information before he made any assurances. Werner said he had met someone he knew only as Herr Schacht. He knew very little about the man.

'And why would this interest me?' said Laumann.

'Because a man with no name is up to something,' said Werner.

'You just said his name is Schacht,' said Laumann.

'I was fishing for a name, so I called him Schacht. To see how he responded.'

'And how did he respond?'

'He pretended it was his name.'

Laumann gave Werner a long look, shook his head in exasperation, but wrote down *Schacht* with a question mark after it. Werner explained they had met in Passau, but Schacht was not from Passau. He was from Munich.

'That isn't much use,' said Laumann.

'He's actually named Walter Meier. He lives in the same

building as one of my customers, a good party man who keeps his eyes open.'

'The customer's name?' said Laumann as he wrote.

'Ballitz,' said Werner. 'Joachim Ballitz.'

'How reliable?' said the SS lieutenant.

'Well, how reliable is anyone?' said Werner.

'And what use is this Meier to me?' said Laumann, playing dumb.

'Meier used a false name,' said Werner. 'He leads a stealthy life. He's up to something.'

'Listen, Krosius. I'm up to my neck in plots. I'm stretched very thin. The closer the invasion gets, the more nervous my colonel gets. He wants this underground operation shut down. Get me something useful from your Ballitz, or I'll put you out of business.'

Werner Krosius just smiled.

The Human Factor

You could take all the security measures you wanted – codes, secret names, arcane procedures – but once you were in the underground, there was no sure-fire protection. The human factor was always there, waiting to trip you up. Something always went wrong – a slip of the tongue, a petty feud, a grudge, a lax moment, a lie, a simple misunderstanding – and then suddenly everything was exposed, and the Gestapo pounced.

By now, the Gestapo and SS had expanded their stations even beyond those Clover knew about. And there were nearly fifty Dachau prison camps, so-called sub-camps, throughout Bavaria. Rosenheim had one. The one in Bad Tölz was less than fifteen kilometers from the hut where Charlie and Elke were waiting. On a clear day, you could just make it out in the distant haze if you knew where to look. Gmund, Tutzing, and a dozen more camps lay between them and the border.

In addition to Charlie's bigotry, another human factor that threatened to get in the way was Joachim Ballitz's love of *foie gras*. Ballitz had wanted to punish Dietrich for stealing the *foie gras*. But how can you punish a fifteen-year-old who runs with a wild crowd and is bigger than you? Once your son knew you weren't going to hit him, the game was pretty much over.

Dietrich made good use of his newfound advantage over his father. Because Joachim detested Elke so vehemently, Dietrich decided to admire her. The old man would go on and on about how she was living in the basement without paying rent, how dirty she was, how her presence was polluting the building; how she was stealing food, he was sure of it, no matter what anyone said. Dietrich would praise Elke in return, just to get his father's goat. 'She's smart, she's beautiful, she knows her way around,' he said. One day, his father was going on about Jews and then started on 'that little black bitch,' and Dietrich yelled at him to shut up.

Joachim's face turned red with rage. 'How dare you! I forbid such disrespectful impudence in my house!'

Dietrich laughed at him.

Joachim said his son had better not be carrying on with that black bitch. 'You'll end up in a concentration camp.'

'That would be just like you, to turn in your own son,' said Dietrich.

'Who said anything about turning you in?' said Joachim. 'I'm talking about turning *her* in.'

'For being black?' said Dietrich.

'For doing whatever she's doing,' said Joachim.

'You don't have any idea what she's doing,' said Dietrich.

Joachim looked hard at Dietrich. 'You tell me, then,' he said. 'What *is* she doing?'

'I don't know,' said Dietrich. 'How should I know? I was just saying . . .'

'But you just told me *I* don't have any idea what she's doing, which means *you do*.'

'No, it doesn't,' said Dietrich. They went back and forth like this a few times, with Dietrich becoming more and more rattled. Until he finally stormed out and slammed the door.

It now seemed to Ballitz that Elke might have enticed his son into some insane adventure. She was years older than Dietrich, but people did all sorts of crazy things these days. And he imagined a scenario where they were involved in a criminal gang. When Werner Krosius showed up after his most recent meeting with Laumann, Joachim offered him the black girl and, to throw the scent off his son, he offered up the warden Adolf Jobst as well. He didn't really know whether either one was up to anything, but he wanted them both to disappear from his life. Denouncing them might just do the trick.

When Krosius asked whether Ballitz knew how Herr Meier fitted into all this, Joachim Ballitz said, 'They're all in it together.' He waved his arms about to indicate a grand conspiracy too complicated for him to put into words.

'And the American pilot?' said Krosius, looking for anything to feed the SS lieutenant.

'The American pilot?' said Ballitz. This was the first time he had heard anything about an American pilot.

'The SS is looking for an American pilot,' said Krosius. 'High-ranking, they think, with critical information about the invasion.'

'Invasion?' said Ballitz, realizing suddenly that his lies and fabrication had led him on to quicksand. 'Oh, I don't know anything about any invasion. Or any American pilot.'

Werner Krosius had gotten more than he could have hoped for from Ballitz. The invasion would happen soon, and when it did, every conspiracy theory would be half right. Krosius reckoned that even an implausible fairy tale would serve his purposes for the immediate future. And if it all turned out not to be true, it would be Ballitz who had given false information, not him. A plausible lie was worth more than the truth. Information only had to *seem* true to be useful. By the time Ballitz's information – or rather Krosius's reconstruction of Ballitz's information – proved to be untrue, it would already have served its purpose. And if it turned out to be true, then so much the better.

Ballitz was very nervous about what he had just said. So Krosius offered him a jar of *foie gras* at a very good price. 'It's first-rate stuff from the French Perigord. I wouldn't do this for everyone,' he said.

Hans Bergemann was one of a few contacts Willi still had in the Munich police department. Willi had asked him about Werner Krosius after Krosius had followed him from Passau. What Bergemann found out seemed worrisome.

'Until about a year ago, Krosius was a small-time operator,' said Bergemann. 'Now he's expanded his business from food and goods to information. He's made his customer base into a network of informers. He's become indispensable to the SS and the Gestapo. The worrisome thing is he knows you, so *they* know you. Not everything, but enough to be dangerous. He's got a customer in your building.'

'Of course,' said Willi, remembering Ballitz and his fancy food.

Clover

The rain drummed mercilessly on the stone roof and poured off the corners in great gushes. Elke sat in her corner of the hut reading a book. Charlie wiped the fog from the window and scowled out at the pasture. Rivulets of water coursed down the hill, over pasture, over stones, around boulders, running together, gathering strength and volume, joining a larger stream that rushed into the forest below. The pasture was vivid green. The lush grass was tall, and it had been knocked flat by the rushing water.

Elke had brought food with her – bread, cheese, sausage, and some cherries the Zoellners had given her. She had also brought tea. She used a small camping stove to heat water. She put the food on the table and took her share back to her corner.

'You can eat at the table,' said Charlie.

'Thanks,' she said. 'I'm fine here.' She went back to reading.

Charlie returned to his silence.

Charlie was trying his best not to be sullen or hostile or anything of the kind. But, damn it, she met every effort he made with indifference and hostility. There was only one path to her good graces, as far as he could figure out, and that was to surrender to her authority. He understood that would be like plowing deep furrows across the graves of his ancestors, leaving desecration and ruined ground behind. His parents would never forgive him. He would never forgive himself.

The border seemed far away, but this – the defeat of his own ignorance and prejudice, the rejection of his own past; no, not just his past, but his here and now – seemed beyond imagining. And the colored girl seemed to delight in his misery.

'What's your name?' said Charlie.

'Clover,' said Elke, without looking up from her book.

'No. I mean your real name.'

'I won't tell you that,' she said.

Not *I can't tell you*, but *I won't tell you*. Her response made him mad. For some reason, he thought of the Red Tails, the black pilots, again. 'You know there are colored pilots in the American Army.'

Elke looked up from her book.

'Black American pilots,' he said.

She did not answer and went back to her book.

What did she want from him? Charlie wondered. He was making every effort to be cordial – against his upbringing, against everything that meant something to him – and she was cold and indifferent.

'Listen, Clover,' he said. He pronounced her name with a sneer, but when she looked up from her book again, he didn't have anything more to say.

'I'm reading,' she said. And she turned back to her book. Then she thought a moment and closed the book with her finger marking the page. 'No. *You* listen, Captain. You and I have to cooperate and work together if we're going to get out of here safely, but we don't have to be friends. Neither one of us even *wants* to be friends.

'Maybe you're sorry you said some of the things you said to me. And, I don't know, maybe you even want to cooperate. Good. But you're not the first white man to curse and abuse me. It's happened over and over, more times than I can count. The things you said were stupid and mean, but I've learned not to let such things hurt me. It's *your* stupidity, *your* hatred. It's *your* problem. It doesn't touch me.'

Even Charlie could see, in that moment, that it *did* touch her. He took some satisfaction from that, and then felt shame for taking satisfaction in hurting her. Still, saying *I'm sorry* was the last thing he could imagine doing.

She said it for him. 'Maybe you're sorry. And now you want to do something about it, something to make things right. Well, you can't. It's done, it can't be . . .' She couldn't find the English. '*Ungetan.*'

'Undone?' said Charlie. 'It can't be undone.'

'Yes. It can't be undone. You want to make yourself feel better. If I'm friendly now, that makes you feel better. Maybe you feel you are doing something good by being friendly. And maybe you think I should be friendly back.' This was exactly what Charlie thought. 'But why should I? You want to feel better, and you think I should help you?' He thought that, too.

'Maybe you think you're having a great awakening. I've seen people change, but I've never seen any great awakenings. People change slow. They change when they work to change. You change by working, not by me working for you. You think talking about black American pilots is work? Why do you want to talk to me about *them*?'

'I thought you would like to know that . . .'

'I am not a pilot, and I am not American.'

'But you are black,' said Charlie.

'And that makes the pilots and me the same?'

'I thought you'd be . . . interested.' That was a lie, and he knew it as he said it.

'Are *you* interested?' she said.

'I am,' said Charlie. 'They're damn good pilots.' Another lie. It even *sounded* like a lie.

'And because you think they're good pilots, you think I should believe in your good intentions?'

'I didn't say that,' said Charlie, getting angrier. But she was right again.

'You didn't have to say it,' said Elke. 'Why should I be interested in black pilots?'

He wanted to lash out again but bit his tongue. Then he gave it one last try. 'Well, you should be proud when your people are good at something.'

She studied him for a long moment before she said, 'You have a lot of work to do, Captain Herder.'

The Hikers

Elke led the way. She walked with a slow and steady step, and Charlie could tell she had hiked in the mountains before. She could maintain that pace indefinitely without getting out of breath, and he got in step four or five meters behind her.

The path had gotten steep right away at the top of the pasture. Then it led on to stony ground and got steeper still. Little yellow wildflowers had come up among the stones across the slope. The few trees and shrubs were short and gnarled. The path was narrow and switched back and forth. They paused after climbing for thirty minutes and turned to look. The hut's roof was visible eight hundred meters below. The temperature had dropped and there was a breeze.

They climbed some more, and after a while the hut and the pasture were out of sight. There were no longer any trees, only boulders and stones. The path became harder to see. Occasionally, there was a faded blaze to indicate a change in direction. An hour and a half out, they found themselves in a vast stone field. There were a few grasses and small wildflowers between the stones, but that was the only growth.

They came upon a marker, an iron crucifix. 'This is where somebody died,' said Elke.

'How do you know?' said Charlie.

'That's what they do in the mountains,' said Elke. 'They mark where somebody died. Maybe a . . . a . . . *eine Lawine*. A snow slide?'

'An avalanche?' said Charlie. He looked up at the steep slope above them.

'Avalanche. Yes,' said Elke. 'Snow. Or stone.'

'Why is your English so good?' said Charlie.

'Because a "colored girl" shouldn't speak good English?' said Elke.

Charlie thought about it for a moment. Maybe that *was* it.

But her saying it made him mad. Everything she did made him mad.

They continued up the mountain. The trail was barely visible, and the blazes had all but disappeared. They came to a small pile of stones where another trail crossed theirs. 'If we have to go this way, this is where we'd turn,' she said, pointing. 'Let's go back.'

It had been a strenuous hike. It was cold, and there was a steady, sharp wind coming across the face of the mountain. The stones were loose. Going down was more difficult than going up. Sometimes their walking would make a stone start rolling down the mountain. It was easy to see how an avalanche might happen.

After what seemed to Charlie like a very long time, the hut came into view below. Elke stopped suddenly and dropped down, signaling with two quick waves of her hand for Charlie to drop, too. 'Two men,' she whispered. She took the binoculars from her rucksack and studied the figures. 'SS,' she said. 'They're trying to get in.'

The wind brought their voices up the mountain, but she couldn't make out what they were saying. The men circled around the hut, trying the door and shutters several times. They were solid and secure, and there was no way in. One of them kicked the door in frustration. Then they sat on the porch smoking. They laughed about something. They ground out their cigarettes on the edge of the porch and dropped the butts. They shouldered their rifles, walked back down the pasture, and disappeared into the woods.

'What now?' said Charlie.

'We wait to be sure they're really gone,' said Elke.

And so they sat there watching for someone to emerge from the forest below. The sun was low in the sky, and then it went behind the mountain, turning everything scarlet and purple. The temperature dropped. Charlie pulled the sheepskin from his rucksack and put it on. The moon rose. It was nearly full. They could still see the hut clearly, the pasture, and the dark forest below. They took turns watching.

It was nearly dark when Clover saw a single figure emerge from the forest and make its way to the hut. She peered down through the binoculars. 'It's Geranium,' she said. 'Let's go.'

Fedor was waiting on the porch. They all went inside. As he unloaded provisions from his rucksack, he told them how the SS had questioned the Zoellners about the summer pasture.

Helga Zoellner told them she hadn't said anything about the *Alm* because they hadn't asked. How could they know about summer pastures? they said. Helga said she couldn't know they didn't know about summer pastures. How could she know what they knew or didn't know? The two SS men seemed mollified but still insisted on going up to the *Alm*. 'The lieutenant,' they said.

Jürgen Zoellner grumbled but took them as far as the forest and gave them directions from there. He sent them by a longer route, the route he used when he was bringing up the cows, but they didn't know that. Geranium came up as soon as he heard from the Zoellners.

Geranium and Clover discussed whether the SS men were likely to return or not, and whether Clover and Charlie would be safe staying in the hut. Geranium thought the SS men would probably not come back. They were lazy and undisciplined. They had left their cigarette butts outside the hut. What kind of soldier did that? In any case, Clover and Charlie should be safe until sunrise.

Clover suggested that they leave early in the day, taking all their things with them, and return in the evening.

The three ate supper without talking further, then slept. The next morning, Charlie, Geranium, and Clover ate the same thing they had eaten the night before: black bread, hard-boiled eggs, and tea.

Geranium was worried. If the invasion didn't come soon, they would have to move on anyway without the diversion the invasion would have offered. The morning was clear and cold. Geranium shook their hands. He held on a little too long for Charlie's liking. Then he went back down the mountain. Clover and Charlie packed their rucksacks, slung them on to their backs, and went back up the mountain. They walked more slowly with the loaded rucksacks than they had the day before.

They climbed for much of the morning, past the iron crucifix, to the trail junction where they took the right turn. Clover said it would be a circuitous route, and it was a difficult trail mostly used by hikers. The advantage, she said, was that there was a hiking hut further along. And no one would be using it this early in the season.

'Who planned the route?' said Charlie.

'Geranium and Dandelion,' said Clover. Geranium was an avid hiker, she said, and knew this part of the country very well.

'He doesn't look it,' said Charlie. 'Like a hiker, I mean.'

They walked on in silence again. Then Clover said, 'We have a plan for the first two days out. Contacts, places to hide. Beyond that, we will have to improvise.'

'How long to the French border?' said Charlie.

'It will be the Swiss border. There's no way to know how long it will take. That depends.'

'How will we know where to cross?'

'There's no way to know that either. We'll have to see when we get there.'

Jesus! he thought. *Amateur hour.* But he kept it to himself.

Charlie found himself wondering about Clover – who she was, where she had come from, how a black girl came to be German. He didn't know there were black Germans. He didn't know Germany had had African colonies. Did they still? He didn't know about the French occupation of the Rhineland.

They stopped to eat lunch by a crude shelter someone had made by stacking stones into a kind of teepee. He wondered whether it had been made as shelter from a storm.

'Maybe,' said Clover.

'I wouldn't trust it,' he said.

Clover didn't say anything.

They ate their black bread, another hard-boiled egg, some cherries. Clover drank from her canteen. Charlie hadn't brought any water, and she didn't offer him any. It was a good thing, too, because he wasn't going to drink from a colored girl's canteen.

June 6, 1944

The Pointe du Hoc is a stony promontory on the Normandy coast. It juts into the sea just to the west of what we now know as Omaha Beach and to the east of Utah Beach. From massive bunkers and reinforced gun emplacements on the Pointe du Hoc and from other vantage points spread out all along above the beaches, the Germans would be able to rain fire down on the beaches below.

On the night of June 5, Allied bombers, flying out of bases in England, began a heavy bombardment on the Normandy coast. But because the weather was overcast and the targets were obscured, they dropped their bombs inland, and the shoreline defenses remained largely intact.

Then, shortly after midnight, several thousand American and British paratroopers were dropped behind the German defenses. And a few hours after that, the beach landings began. Despite the increased radio chatter and the air attacks, Hitler was not expecting the invasion there. He was sure that any activity in Normandy was a ruse, that the real invasion would eventually come at Calais.

General Erwin Rommel thought all along it would be Normandy. He had been preparing for many months. He had built massive reinforced concrete bunkers and gun emplacements all along the shore, and particularly at Pointe du Hoc.

The morning of June 6 was stormy, as the night before had been. Rommel, believing an attack unlikely because of the weather, had gone to Germany to celebrate his wife's birthday. Daylight came slowly and dimly, so that those on watch could not at first believe what they were seeing. Stretching across the entire horizon were more ships than anyone could even imagine: battleships, light and heavy cruisers, destroyers, and escorts by the thousands. This was the largest naval invasion in the history of the world. And as the first ships came within range, they began firing their big guns at the German gun emplacements on the

Pointe du Hoc and elsewhere. The German guns fired back. Landing craft began ferrying Allied soldiers toward shore. Before long, the sea was full of landing craft.

Because of their configuration, the landing craft, or LSTs (for their naval designation – Landing Ship, Tank), were hard to maneuver in the heavy water. They came slowly, drifting off course, and arriving wherever they could. They were also sitting ducks. Those that made it close to shore dropped their ramps, and the soldiers ran down into the surging tide. Many found themselves in deep water too far from shore. Some drowned, pulled under by the heavy equipment they carried, or were shot by raking machine gun fire from the German heights. Others made it to the beach only to get tangled in Rommel's obstacles. But many made it on to the beach where they got up against the cliffs.

The machine-gun fire was non-stop; mortar shells and grenades and heavy artillery rained down on them from above. In the first hours, thousands were killed, thousands more wounded. The Germans took heavy casualties, too. The Allies kept coming ashore and started making their way up on to the cliffs and hills. They used ropes and grappling hooks and ladders. They hurled grenades at the bunkers on the hilltops. They were driven back, killed, and others took their place.

'Herr General, the invasion has begun.'

General Friedrich Dollmann sat up in bed. His chief of staff switched on the light. The chief handed him the report and he read it. 'A thousand ships?' said Dollmann. 'That can't be.'

'Probably more,' said the adjutant. Dollmann, the commander of Germany's Seventh Army, was running war games in Rennes, far from the invasion. There was little he could do where he was.

As soon as General Rommel received the invasion report, he got the German High Command on the phone. He insisted on immediate reinforcements; Panzer divisions were waiting in reserve for just such a moment.

Any reinforcements would have to be okayed by the Führer, was the reply. So get the Führer's OK, said Rommel. *He's asleep*, was the reply. 'And the Führer has given explicit orders not to be woken on any account.'

Hitler was at Berghof, his mountain retreat in Bavaria, not too far from the mountain where Charlie and Clover were waiting. By the time he finally got out of bed – it was around noon – the 75th Rangers were on Pointe du Hoc dropping thermite grenades into the works of the German's big 155-millimeter guns.

The Atlantic Wall had been breached, and a beachhead had been established. Huge floating docks were being maneuvered into place, and trucks, tanks, arms, and men were coming ashore by the thousands. Safe routes inland had been established on several roads, and a continuous stream of men and machines poured up the roads.

Hitler saw no reason to doubt that this was the feint he had predicted all along. He refused to talk to his generals, who, to his mind, were either cowards or idiots. He declined to send reinforcements to Normandy.

By day's end, 34,000 invading soldiers were on shore and on the heights.

Day after day, Willi and Lola had listened, like millions of others, to the BBC. The signal was full of static and jamming noises, and they had to keep the volume low. But the BBC was the only reliable source for news. In fact, the German High Command listened to find out what was really going on; the German broadcasts were nothing but wishful thinking and patriotic nonsense.

The BBC broadcasts were interspersed with coded messages – particular pieces of music for the Polish resistance, snippets of poetry for the French. On the first day of June, the first three lines of Paul Verlaine's 'Chanson D'Automne' had been repeated over and over again: *Les saglots longs des violons de l'automne* (The long sobs of the violins of autumn), a signal to the French resistance that the invasion was coming soon. Four days later, the next three lines were broadcast: *Blessent mon coeur d'une langueur monotone* (Injure my heart with a monotonous languor), meaning the invasion was imminent.

Early on June 6, Willi and Lola were having breakfast when the BBC broke into its program with a news bulletin. Several thousand paratroopers had jumped into France the night before. Willi closed his eyes for a moment to let the news sink in. 'What is it?' said Lola.

'Paratroopers in France,' said Willi. 'The invasion is underway.'

'Are you sure?'

The BBC announcement of the invasion came a little later that morning: 'D-Day has come,' said the announcer. 'Early this morning, the Allies began the assault on the north-western face of Hitler's European fortress. The first official news came just after half-past nine, when the Supreme Headquarters of the Allied Expeditionary Force . . . issued Communiqué Number One. This said: "Under the command of General Eisenhower, Allied naval forces, supported by strong air forces, began landing Allied armies this morning on the northern coast of France."'

The plan was for Willi to meet Pierre at five in the evening the day of the invasion. They would drive south to Bessingen where Clover and Charlie were supposed to arrive after dark. Lola was to meet Bergemann at noon to let him know Willi's whereabouts and plans. And Bergemann would tell her about any renewed interest in them by the police or Gestapo. It was possible that the invasion might provoke the SS or the Gestapo in their direction.

Werner Krosius listened to the BBC news bulletin, too. He drank down his coffee, then made two telephone calls to get things started. The drive to Murnau took him two hours.

The Abattoir

Willi watched what was left of Munich go by as Pierre threaded the car through rubble-strewn streets, past ruined factories and apartment buildings. The rail yards were smoldering, and train wagons lay on their sides where they had been tossed by the previous night's bombing.

Once past the city, Pierre picked up speed. The car was a Mercedes with an unfamiliar insignia stenciled on the sides and, from the sound of it, a big engine under the hood. The back seat, where Willi sat, was spacious, with plush seats and a footrest. The window between the back seat and driver was down. Willi had brought a bouquet of flowers, and it lay on the seat beside him. He did that sometimes. If they were stopped, he could claim to be visiting someone's grave in a nearby cemetery.

Willi had a Luger under his jacket, and Pierre was armed, too. 'Whose car?' said Willi, certain that Pierre wouldn't tell him.

'A man,' said Pierre.

On a long, straight stretch of road, they encountered a convoy of tanks and pulled off to let them pass.

'Probably going to France,' said Pierre.

'Too late,' said Willi. It was a good guess. Hitler's generals – first von Schweppenberg, then von Runstedt – pleaded with Hitler to be allowed to withdraw their armies to the Seine where they could regroup and counterattack. Hitler fired them both.

The day was gray. Poppies were nodding along the roadside, their bright blossoms like a thousand little lamps. Willi opened the window. The countryside was splendid, green and lush. The air was fragrant. The hay had recently been cut and stacked across the fields. It would dry there and then be loaded on wagons and carried to the barn.

The Bessingen safe house had once been an abattoir, and the adjoining house had been the residence of the manager. The abattoir was no longer in use, and the dwelling had stood empty for the ten years since the owner had died. The heirs had tried to sell it. But no one was interested in buying it, and it had fallen into disrepair. Windows were broken, the roof leaked in several places, and the wooden floor was rotting. The only people who went inside were lovers and secret drinkers.

Liesl the hotel maid, known to Willi as Daisy, was friends with one of the heirs. Daisy had written to Willi that her friend had expressed interest in their cause. She was fearful for her family's safety but willing at least to let them use the abattoir. The location thirty kilometers northwest of Konstanz and the Swiss border was ideal. Still, Willi wanted to visit the place to make sure everything was as secure as Daisy's friend had promised.

Bessingen's main street went steeply downhill through a horse-shoe curve from one end of the village to the other. The church and cemetery were at the top of the curve and the abattoir was at the bottom.

Pierre parked by the cemetery. From there, they walked down through the village. The rain had stopped. They met no one. The upper part of the horseshoe was lined with small houses. Occasionally, you caught a glimpse between the houses of the abattoir below.

The lot was full of weeds, bushes, and small trees. A wide, black door, big enough for a truck, took up the front of the building. The residence at the back of the building was accessible by a narrow path now strewn with bottles and trash. The door to the house was broken, and they pushed their way inside. There were no cobwebs in the doorway. Willi took a piece of blue yarn from his pocket and tied it on the doorknob. Inside, the house was dusty, but there was no debris, no furniture of any kind, no bottles or cigarette butts. The place had recently been tidied up.

Willi and Pierre were in the back room and were studying the view from the window when they heard someone push the front door open. Pierre reached for the pistol in his belt, but Willi signaled for him to wait. A moment later, a young woman came into the room. 'Are you . . .?' she said. She didn't quite know how to finish the sentence.

'You were expecting someone?' said Willi.

'No. Well, yes. Someone. I mean. Well, Liesl is my friend. She told me . . . I said I'd help.'

She saw Pierre roll his eyes. 'I'm sorry,' she said. 'I've never done anything like this. I mean . . .'

'You should stop talking,' said Willi, and she did. 'Did you see us come in?'

She walked to the back window and pointed up at the house just above. 'I saw you come into town. That's my house. I knew someone was coming, so I was watching.'

'Who else knows someone is coming?'

'Nobody.'

'Your husband?'

'No.'

'Liesl?'

'No. Not from me. Nobody.'

'Who cleaned up here?' said Willi.

'I did.'

'By yourself?' said Willi.

'Yes. I shouldn't have, should I? It's just it was so dirty . . .'

'It doesn't matter,' he said. 'How long have you been watching closely?'

'The last week or so.'

'Has anyone visited the house?'

'No. No one.'

'You're sure?'

'Yes.'

'How can you be sure?'

Willi could see she was confused and terrified. After all, she wanted to help a little, but not so much that she could get in trouble. That was a miscalculation a lot of people made. For the Gestapo, there was no helping a little. You were out or you were in. Making the house available would land her and her husband in Dachau. All this dawned on her at the same moment. It was as though a dam burst. Her eyes filled with tears.

Willi waited while she wept. He did not try to comfort her. When he thought she could listen, he said, 'We will all leave here together now. We'll walk up to your house. We're looking to buy the abattoir, but we didn't give you our names. That will be your story, if you're asked. But you should stop watching.

And stay away from the house altogether. The best thing would be to leave for a week.'

'My sister lives in Munich,' she said, as if Willi had thrown her a life preserver.

'Go this afternoon. With your husband,' said Willi. 'Take the train. Keep your ticket stubs.'

'Yes,' she said. 'Yes, yes.'

Aunt Sally

Geranium knocked on the door of the hut. Charlie opened it. 'The Americans are in Normandy,' Geranium said. 'Normandy, not Calais.' He seized Charlie's hand and pumped it, as though he had just won the lottery. Charlie grinned. He wanted to hear more. Geranium told him what he knew, which wasn't much. There had been massive bombing along the coast the night before. Thousands of paratroopers had been dropped behind the German defenses. A gigantic armada was unloading men on to the beaches by the thousands.

Clover and Charlie stuffed their things into their rucksacks and went outside. The day was overcast and silent.

At the same moment as they were setting off, Jürgen Zoellner started moving his cows. He opened the fence. The lead cow knew where they were going and eagerly came out on to the road, her bell clanging. She remembered the grass of the high meadow. The other cows followed. Twenty-two were making the trip. Two remained behind. They were old and would be going to the slaughterhouse.

The cows followed along the road into the village. They wanted to stop and graze on the lush grass beside the road. The dog ran beside them to keep them moving. Then she ran ahead to turn them up the small road between the church and the cemetery. It led between hayfields and into the dark pine forest. The cows knew the turn. They knew they were going where the grass was lush and deep.

If the SS decided to come up to the *Alm* again, they would find only Jürgen or Helga, and the dog and cows. Jürgen was pretty sure the SS would have other things to keep them busy, now that the Americans had come ashore. He took the cows up the longer route, the way he had shown the SS. At the same time, Charlie, Geranium, and Clover were coming down the more direct way through the thickest and steepest part of the forest.

The rain had made the path into a small stream. They could

still use the path by stepping from stone to stone. You had to be careful because the stones could be slippery. Geranium didn't look like much of a hiker, but he carried a walking stick and used it to pick his way along with skill and speed. Clover picked up a slim pine branch, broke it to length, and began to use it the same way. After Charlie slipped and almost fell, he did the same thing.

The day was overcast, and in the thick of the forest, among the towering firs and pines and spruces, it was almost as dark as night. The only sounds were the call of an occasional cuckoo and the water tumbling over the rocks. Eventually, their stream joined another larger stream, and there was a better path beside it. Soon they crossed the larger stream on a bridge made of two split logs laid side by side. There was a wooden crucifix – one of those Bavarian things that got on Lieutenant Laumann's nerves – just on the other side.

'Let's stop here,' said Geranium. 'We're a little ahead of schedule.'

Charlie hadn't been aware there was a schedule. But he didn't ask because he knew they wouldn't tell him. They didn't tell him anything. And he wondered whether they might just decide to turn him over to the SS. You never knew what was going on with these people.

'We don't want to get there before dark,' said Geranium.

They sat on stones beside the stream and watched the water spill downhill. Nobody talked. Charlie thought about the hut that he would never see again and was surprised that he felt a longing for it.

Looking up, he could barely see any sky. He leaned against the rough trunk of a gigantic pine. When you are in an unfamiliar place in a situation you never expected to be in, with people you do not know and yet are dependent on for your life, it should not be surprising if your mind comes untethered and goes in unfamiliar directions. Charlie was not asleep, but he was dreaming all the same. Geranium and Clover spoke now and then in low tones. Charlie wasn't interested in what they said and made no effort to understand it. His Aunt Sally came to mind.

Sally Bell, the wife of Charlie's mother's brother, had been banished from the family for so long that Charlie had all but forgotten her. As he remembered her now with affection, he realized that he was supposed to feel revulsion instead.

Clifford, Charlie's uncle, had brought Sally home with him after serving in France in the Great War. Her name had been Celine then. Sally had French ways. She was independent, even defiant when it suited her.

Charlie stayed with Uncle Clifford and Aunt Sally the summer he was four. And while Clifford was at work at the mill, Sally took Charlie to the playground. She pushed Charlie on the swing. 'Higher!' he said. 'Higher!' He climbed on the jungle gym and played in the sandbox. He played with another little boy about his age – Reginald – and over time they became friends. Charlie would ask Aunt Sally if Reginald would be at the park today. 'I hope so,' he said.

Charlie was too young to notice that Reginald was a colored boy. But word got to his mother and father what he had done, and, worse, what Sally had done. His father spanked Charlie for playing with a colored boy, said he should know better, and it had better not happen again. Sally was not banished right away, but that was when it started.

That was probably not the first moment in Charlie's racist education. And certainly many similar moments had followed, anchoring his bigotry ever more firmly in the fundament of his being. Urged by his family and his experience, he had driven first Reginald and then Sally from his consciousness. Neither made sense any more in the context of his life.

He could not summon any memory of the boy besides his name, and even that was tainted and came with difficulty. But Aunt Sally had sprung apparently vividly to mind as though she were nearby, or at least something *about her* was nearby. He remembered her crime, but at the same time he remembered how he had loved her, her perfume, her smile, how she hugged him and kissed him. She had more warmth about her than the rest of his family put together. 'Aunt Sally.' He must have said it aloud because Clover and Geranium looked at him.

Geranium looked at his watch then and stood up. 'Time to go,' he said. Clover got up, too, and then so did Charlie. They put on their rucksacks and started downhill again. They picked their way along and, after another hour, emerged from the forest just above the Zoellner winter pasture, with its barns and fences. The house was visible a few hundred meters down the road. Further along was the town with its fine church steeple, and beyond that, in the distance, the towering snowcapped Alps.

As they approached, Helga came out of the barn and climbed into the back of the truck parked by the barn. The truck had high tin sides lined with wood planks, a wooden floor, and a tin roof. It was divided lengthwise into two stalls. Inside on the front and side walls were heavy iron hooks with ropes to hold livestock in place. Helga twisted two latches at the top of the front wall, then tugged hard on the hooks, and the top half of the wall came away, revealing a narrow space behind the cab that was invisible when the wall was in place.

'For you,' she said, pointing to Charlie.

What's Funny?

The ride from the Zoellners' to the abattoir was a hundred and ninety kilometers. If things went smoothly, it would take four hours. They would be going north, then west, then south, avoiding military installations and SS outposts. They had thought at first they would keep to small roads, but Willi had said that the only reason for a truck from elsewhere to be on small roads was to avoid attracting attention. On the busier highways, they could blend in with whatever traffic there was. There wouldn't be much, a few trucks and military convoys was all. And even if they were stopped or came to a checkpoint, they had a bill of sale and orders to deliver the two cows to a commercial slaughterhouse near Konstanz.

After they delivered the cows, they would drive the few kilometers back to the Bessingen safe house. The next morning before sunrise, Clover and Charlie would make their way on foot to a rendezvous with partisans who would escort them over the border. The border in Konstanz was heavily guarded and patrolled, and too dangerous. But the partisans would take them where they would be able to cross.

Charlie and Clover climbed into the secret compartment. Once the false back was in place, it was too dark for them to see anything, but they could still hear what was going on outside. Helga led the two cows into the truck and tied them in place. They were snorting and bellowing and breathing loudly and stamping around. Helga closed the tailgate and latched it in place. A short while later, they heard the truck doors open and close, and Geranium said from the front right seat, 'Everything all right back there?'

'Yes, everything's good,' said Clover.

'Captain?' said Geranium.

'Good,' said Charlie.

Helga started the engine and put the truck in gear. The cows moved around uneasily. The truck started with a lurch, the cows moved around some more, one bellowed, and then they were rolling forward. The truck rocked and shuddered as they came out of the barnyard, but once they were on pavement, the ride got smoother, and the cows calmed down. It was an old truck, made for farm use and short-distance travel, so the suspension system was stiff and magnified every bump in the road.

They rode without speaking. Only Helga spoke. To ease her mind, she talked about what she saw. 'Wegener needs to cut his hay. He'll lose it if he waits too long.' Or: 'That guy's slow,' when they were driving behind a tractor. 'C'mon on, move it.' Sometimes she hummed snatches of unrecognizable tunes. She also had the habit of waving to people they passed.

Before very long, they encountered their first military convoy. There would be several more. The invasion may have been a useful diversion, but it had also stirred things up, like poking a stick in a hornets' nest. So the army was restless and out and about.

They stopped at a crossroads as a convoy rolled past: motor-cycles, half-tracks, and trucks full of soldiers. Charlie and Clover sat in the dark and listened to truck after truck going by. Helga waved as the last truck passed and a soldier waved back. That made Geranium nervous, but he didn't say anything.

Charlie and Clover were aware of one another's presence in the dark. Their legs or their shoulders would touch sometimes when the truck swayed or lurched. 'Sorry,' Charlie said the first few times it happened, but then he stopped. Clover fell asleep once, and Charlie could tell. At one point, she relaxed against his side, but when she woke up, she straightened up and moved away as best she could. Once when Charlie fell asleep, his head lolled over against Clover's shoulder. She tried to move away, but there was no place to go so she just let him sleep. When he woke up, he said 'Sorry.'

'That's OK,' she said.

Clover had first heard about the Flower Gang from one of the restaurant cooks who gave her food. He had asked her to take a package to someone hiding in a nearby basement. Herr Bernstorf, the cook who gave her the package, told her what she was doing was dangerous, but it was important work and would help people who needed help. If anyone asked who gave her the package, she should say Nasturtium. She wondered whether it was because the nasturtium was an edible flower, and he had laughed.

As someone who needed help herself, Clover liked the idea of helping people who needed help. And as someone whose life was continually under threat, she was not put off by the danger. Herr Bernstorf was a half-Jew, so he was probably in more danger than she was, and he didn't let that stop him.

Nasturtium directed her toward Dandelion, whom she already knew as Herr Meier, a tenant in the building where she lived. She had sorted out the theft of Ballitz's *foie gras*, and after that Frau Meier had vouched for her. And now here she was in the back of a cattle truck, trying to save the life of a man who hated her. Well, that was the way life turned out sometimes. She had to laugh.

'What's funny?' said Charlie.

'Nothing.'

'Then why'd you laugh?'

'No reason,' she said. Then she decided to tell him.

'I don't hate you,' he said.

She didn't answer. The truck was noisy, and he didn't know if she heard him, so he said it again.

'I heard you,' she said.

Neither one spoke for a long time.

'Why did you join the army, Captain?' said Clover.

'To fly. I wanted to fly,' said Charlie.

'So it didn't have anything to do with stopping Hitler,' said Clover.

'Sure,' said Charlie, unsure of where this line of conversation was coming from or where it would take him. 'Sure. We have to stop Hitler.'

'Why? What's Hitler to you? You and Hitler have some of the same ideas.'

So that's it, thought Charlie. *Race*. 'It's always about race with you, isn't it?' said Charlie. Every time anything came up, she threw race in his face.

'It's *never* about race with me,' she said. 'I'm helping save your skinny white ass. What are you doing for me?'

Charlie thought about it for a moment. 'I'm letting you save my skinny white ass.' They sat in silence for a moment, letting the truth of the moment sink in, then they both started laughing. And then they couldn't stop.

'Everything all right back there?' said Geranium.

'Yes,' said Clover. 'Everything's all right.'

'We're good,' said Charlie.

They ate the hard-boiled eggs they had brought with them in silence. Once in a while, Charlie heard Clover chuckle, and then he had to laugh, too.

The Roadblock

'Roadblock just ahead,' said Geranium. 'Four soldiers, two motorcycles. And dogs.' Helga had papers – hers and those for the slaughterhouse – on the seat beside her. Fedor had identification in his hand proving he was Fedor Matjek, a farm worker. He let Clover and Charlie know what was going on. 'There are maybe a dozen cars ahead of us. They've just made the people in the front car get out. Two soldiers are looking inside front and back. The ones with the dogs are just standing by. They're opening the trunk. They're moving things around. Now they've closed it. They're waving the car through.'

The cars passed through pretty easily one after the other. The small truck ahead of them was another matter. It was a panel truck with the name of an electrical firm on the sides and back. The driver had to get out. He had to open the back of the truck, and two soldiers got in with one of the dogs.

'What are they looking for?' Helga said.

'This close to the border, I'd guess it's people: Jews, others,' said Fedor. 'And us.'

After what seemed like a long time, the soldier with the dog got out of the truck and closed the rear doors. He nodded to the sergeant standing with the driver. The sergeant gave the driver back his papers. The driver got back in his truck and drove off.

The sergeant waved for Helga to drive forward, which she did.

All four policemen walked to the truck, two on each side.

'*Grüß Gott!*' said Helga.

'Papers,' said the sergeant in charge, and stuck out his hand. Helga passed her papers out to him, along with Fedor's. The sergeant studied them, looked from the photo to Helga, then from Fedor's photo to him. Then he studied the bill from the slaughterhouse, turning it over, studying the stamps and the signatures. 'Step out of the truck and open the back,' he said

Helga and Fedor got out. Being the farm worker, Fedor went back and lifted and swung the heavy iron latch to the side, opening the tailgate. The cows stamped and snorted. This started the dogs barking, which started the cows bellowing. The soldiers handling the dogs pulled them away from the truck and held the leashes tight. The dogs stopped barking.

'You need to get those cows out so we can look around,' said the sergeant.

'Do you have a ramp?' said Fedor.

The sergeant just looked at Fedor. Finally, he nodded to one of the soldiers and said, 'Ziegler, get up inside and look around.'

Ziegler was not happy. The truck was barely wide enough for the two cows. Once Ziegler was in the truck, there was no place for him to go. When he tried to edge by on one side, the cow tried to turn its head and started moving around nervously, bellowing and pushing Ziegler hard up against the side wall.

'What do you see, Ziegler?' said the sergeant.

'Cows and cow shit,' said Ziegler. The other soldiers laughed.

'Come down, Ziegler. Close it up,' said the sergeant, and Fedor did.

As they were walking back to the front, it occurred to the sergeant to look under the truck. But all he saw was the driveshaft and urine and manure oozing between the floorboards. He made a disgusted face, handed their papers back to Helga, and waved them to go ahead.

Helga started the engine, put it in gear, and they drove off.

Charlie and Clover had heard most of it. Clover reached for her canteen, unscrewed the top, and drank. The water was no longer cold, and it tasted metallic from the canteen. She held it out toward Charlie. 'Here,' she said.

Charlie was thirsty, and after a moment's hesitation, he reached out and took the canteen and drank deeply. He screwed the lid back on and passed it back to Clover. 'Thank you,' he said.

It would have been hard for Charlie to explain, but something had shifted for him. He found himself in an unfamiliar state of mind, a new place. Maybe he had been there all along, ever since the Mustang had dumped him out into the night sky. Maybe it had just taken him this long to recognize it, to catch up with where he actually was.

His old reality had been levered aside by a new reality, where a hard-boiled egg was a feast, where laughter bound you to someone, and where a drink of water was just a drink of water. Sitting here, jammed into that hot, narrow space with Clover was somehow an event worthy of note. Oddly enough, Clover was thinking the same thing.

Chocolate

The cows were delivered to the slaughterhouse on the northern outskirts of Konstanz. It was a large operation, and since all meat production was controlled by the state, there were military inspectors receiving all shipments. Even a shipment of just two old cows had to be signed in, permits had to be certified, receipts had to be issued. That was something Fedor hadn't counted on when he had planned the operation.

He stood by and watched as workers went about their business. They opened the back of the truck. They went in, squeezed by the cows, and untied their halters from the hooks that had held them in place. At that point, they were so close that Charlie and Clover could hear one of them muttering as he wrestled with a knot.

They heard the ropes being slid from the hooks. Workers backed the cows out on to the loading dock, while two officials – a government inspector and a military inspector – watched the entire operation. The inspectors looked over the paperwork to be sure it matched the cows, and then issued the receipts.

The focus was on meat and not illegal human cargo. There was little danger that Clover and Charlie would be discovered. Everything proceeded as it was supposed to. And after getting the receipts, Helga and Fedor got back in the truck and drove Clover and Charlie off into the night.

The drive to Bessingen took forty minutes. It was nearly midnight, and the town was dark. Helga left them just outside the town. Fedor, Elke, and Charlie watched her drive away. The moon was nearly full. It lit their way down the empty street to the abattoir. They found their way through the bushes, and through the back door.

The plan had been that Geranium would return home with Helga, but he had announced at the last minute that he would stay the night and see them through meeting the people taking them across the border. He had been instrumental in setting up the meeting, and so he thought it made sense that he should go along at least as far as the meeting. He said he would make his way home from there.

They made themselves as comfortable as they could on the floor, with their backs against the wall. Geranium said they should try to get some sleep. But they would be leaving at first light in just a few hours, and sleep seemed out of the question.

The plan was that they were to walk to a rendezvous point west of Bessingen. 'We should eat something,' said Geranium. He took black bread, some boiled potatoes, and sausage out of his rucksack. Clover took out her knife and cut the bread.

'*Verdammt!*' said Clover. She held out her hand. You could see in the dim light that it was bleeding. 'That was stupid,' she said.

Geranium tried to have a look.

'It's nothing,' she said. But it wasn't nothing. It was a deep cut, and it was bleeding badly.

Charlie went into his rucksack and found the first-aid kit he still had from the Mustang. He splashed water from her canteen on the cut, washed her hand, patted it dry, and put iodine on the cut. It burned, and she made a face. He pressed a folded gauze on it. 'Hold this,' he said. 'Press it hard.' He tore off several strips of adhesive tape and taped the gauze in place. He took her hand and raised it over her head. 'Hold your hand up like this. It'll help stop the bleeding.' They sat side by side, and whenever she lowered her hand, Charlie would lift it up.

They heard Geranium snoring softly. They sat in silence.

'Do you like the danger?' said Charlie, almost without meaning to.

Clover was startled, maybe just by the sound of his voice, since they had been silent for so long. Geranium continued to snore. 'No,' she said finally without looking his way. 'I don't like the danger.'

'I do,' said Charlie. 'Well, not the danger exactly. But what the danger has done for me.'

Now Clover looked at him. 'What has it done for you?'

'Well,' said Charlie. Now he had to explain, and he didn't know if he could. 'It feels like it's given me something. In a way,' he added, embarrassed by the grandiosity of his declaration.

'I don't know. It's made me free, made me *feel* free.' He might
have said, *It has given me you*, but he didn't know that yet.
Anyway, she would have misunderstood anything of that sort as
some kind of crazy declaration of love or something, and that
was not what he meant. But he couldn't say exactly *what* he
meant, so he just stopped talking.

They sat in silence some more. She rummaged around inside
her rucksack for a while. Finally, she found a small flat package
and held it out toward him. 'Chocolate,' she said.

'Wow!' said Charlie. 'Where'd you get that?'

'From a chef,' she said.

Charlie broke off a piece and handed it back to her. She broke
off a piece. They both sat in silence, chewing the chocolate slowly
into small pieces, letting it melt in their mouths, letting its deli-
ciousness flood over their tongues, feeling the tiny but irresistible
happiness that comes from eating chocolate.

'Can I ask you a personal question?' said Charlie.

She didn't answer.

'How did you learn such good English? No, I'm not joking.
I mean it.'

'I was a singer,' she said finally. 'With a band in a club. We
did all the American hits.' She gazed into the darkness as she
remembered.

'Name a hit,' she said. 'Something you like.'

Charlie thought for a moment. 'Beyond the Blue Horizon,' he
said.

She started to sing softly. Her speaking voice was low and
husky, but she sang with a soft, sweet soprano.

>Beyond the blue horizon
>Waits a beautiful day
>Goodbye to things that bore me
>Joy is waiting for me.
>
>I see a new horizon
>My life has only begun
>Beyond the blue horizon
>Lies a rising sun.

When she stopped, the silence that swept over them was hard to bear. They sat there beside one another for a long minute. Geranium continued to snore.

'Don't forget to hold your arm up,' said Charlie.

She did as she was told.

Laumann Reports

SS Lieutenant Laumann hated reporting to the commandant of his SS group, SS Colonel Kurt Strang. First of all, it meant going to Munich, which Laumann hated. Munich for him was Bavaria in spades.

Furthermore, he and the colonel did not like one another. Strang found Laumann too ambitious, too eager to please. And Laumann felt that Strang was never satisfied with his reports. Strang invariably said something like 'Is that really all you have, Laumann? What the devil have you been up to down there?'

But this time, Laumann was sure he had something big enough to impress the colonel. He clicked his heels together and saluted. '*Herr Oberst!*' he said, almost shouting, so that Strang sat back in his chair. '*Herr Oberst*, we have uncovered the heart of the conspiracy that I have previously reported on. We are about to arrest the lot of them.'

'Conspiracy, Laumann? What conspiracy? I can't be expected to remember every small detail that crosses my desk.'

Laumann was not deterred. 'There is, as you well know, a widespread conspiracy, *Herr Oberst*, that has been operating in Bavaria, smuggling enemies of the state, Jews, internal enemies, and enemy pilots across the Swiss and French borders in numbers. They have also been engaged in sabotage against the Reich, and in the black market to a massive extent. Until now, they have succeeded in eluding authority.'

'Well, that would be your fault, wouldn't it, Lieutenant?'

Laumann should have known that was coming. He did his best to ignore it and press on. '*Herr Oberst*, thanks to my network of informants . . .'

'I always thought your network of informants was a waste of time . . .'

'Thanks to my network of informants, *Herr Oberst*, I have discovered that the leader of this massive conspiracy is none other than a former police detective named Willi Geismeier.

Geismeier has long been sought by the Gestapo for the murder of an SS *Oberst*' – Laumann paused for effect – 'an SS *Oberst*, *Herr Oberst*, and for other crimes against the Reich. Geismeier operates out of an apartment building in Munich, right under your nose, *Herr Oberst*.'

Colonel Strang remained silent.

'I have also learned the identities of two members of this conspiracy, and from these members we will soon learn about the rest and bring them all to justice. I have also learned that a plot is in motion as we speak to transport an American pilot and intelligence officer out of the country. I have been in touch with Gestapo headquarters, and now I am reporting all this to you, *Herr Oberst*.'

'Is there more?' said Colonel Strang.

There was more. The Gestapo had now joined his investigation. They had pieced together bits of information provided by Ballitz in Munich – some of it true, some of it invented. Werner Krosius had provided crucial information, although Laumann did not mention Krosius by name. That had been their agreement. Even interviews with Egon Scharfheber the beer-truck driver and Sepp Krupke the waiter had yielded small pieces in the puzzle. They knew about Liesl the waitress, also known as Daisy. They knew about Fedor, also known as Geranium, and his connection to Geismeier.

Before leaving Munich, Elke had noticed the Ballitz boy sniffing around. And then one day he had approached her, saying he knew what she was up to and he wanted to be part of it. 'I've seen you with old Herr Meier,' he said. She understood that he may have seen her with Dandelion, but she was sure he was making up the rest of it.

'You're mistaken,' she said. 'You're imagining things.'

'No, I'm not,' said Dietrich. 'I could turn you in, you know.'

'Yes, you could. And you would be making a big mistake, because the first name I'd mention would be yours.'

'My father buys shit on the black market, you know. I could give you him.'

Hearing that, she turned and walked away.

'That boy is dangerous,' she told Willi at the time. It turned out he was.

Everybody was. There was no one revealing moment. Instead, it was a puzzle made of tiny bits of information, some of it true, much of it false, and each bit too small to amount to anything by itself. But put together with something else equally insignificant, suddenly it all amounted to something. Colonel Kurt Strang had no choice but to thank Laumann for his report and offer his congratulations on a job well done.

Ernst Nutzke

Fedor woke up at first light. He wasn't sure whether he had heard Clover singing, or whether he had dreamed it. She and Charlie were both awake. Charlie had just helped Clover change the bandage on her hand.

They all three put on their rucksacks and left the house. Clover took the blue yarn from the doorknob. They walked one at a time down the road as far as the river. Clover went first and waited for the others under the bridge. After a few minutes, Charlie went; then, after a few more minutes, Geranium went.

From there they followed the river upstream. The day was cloudy, and the forest remained dark even after sunrise. The river made a pleasant burbling sound. Once in a while, they heard the coo of a mourning dove.

Rounding a bend in the river, they came upon a man fishing. He looked up as they passed. He smiled and whispered, '*Guten Morgen*,' and then, 'Trout.' There were already three swimming in his bucket.

After an hour, the path took them away from the river and deeper into the forest, just as they had been told it would. They were to follow this path for another hour. Then the path would cross a road. They would come to a tall wire fence with a sign announcing the Frauenberg Hunting Club and a second sign warning against trespassing.

When they got to the hunting club, Clover untied a small piece of blue yarn from the sign and put it in her pocket.

They climbed over a stile – three steps up and down – and went into a dense pine forest. Ferns as high as their hips lined the trail. With every breeze, the ferns moved like the waves of a green sea.

They were supposed to come to a hunting cabin after twenty minutes. Four men would be waiting there to take them the rest of the way. Elke supposed that some of the border with Switzerland would still be porous, as it had been when she had lived in

Konstanz. She figured you would still be able to cross around Schaffhausen. Schaffhausen was the only part of Switzerland north of the Rhine River, so they would be able to cross the border without having to cross the river.

A few minutes along the trail, six men stepped out of the trees and waded through the ferns on to the path. They wore hunting jackets, hats, and boots, and had rifles slung over their shoulders.

'*Grüß Gott*,' they said, smiling. One man – Ernst Nutzke – said, 'Fox,' which was the password. Except he didn't wait for Clover to first say, 'Hunting pheasant?' That was how passwords worked. And they weren't at the cabin where they were supposed to meet. And there were six instead of four. This was all wrong.

Ernst Nutzke had been a criminal all his life. He had gotten thrown out of school for fighting, then he had brawled in the streets with the brown shirts. He had spent two years in prison for criminal assault by the time he was twenty. The army had rejected him because of his criminal record, but the *Zollgrenzschutz*, the German border guards, weren't so choosy.

The work wasn't that hard. Once in a while, you got to beat somebody up. But the smuggling – art, drugs, money – that was the real attraction. And anyone that got in Ernst's way was easy to deal with. All he had to do was say they were crossing illegally. He had shot more than one troublemaker. One had shot back, which was why Ernst walked with a limp.

When it came to smuggling, Ernst was a small operator compared to Werner Krosius. But like most smugglers, he knew who Krosius was and knew how to make himself useful when there was something to gain. Krosius had sought him out for an operation. 'This will interest you,' Krosius said. There was money to be made.

'How much?' said Ernst.

'A thousand,' said Krosius.

All Ernst had to do was intercept a couple of partisans in the forest who were taking a downed American pilot to the Swiss border. They would probably be unarmed. Just arrest them and turn them over to the SS who would be waiting nearby.

'Why don't the SS arrest them?' said Ernst.

'This is how they want to do it,' said Krosius. 'Don't you want it? I can get somebody else.'

'No, I want it,' said Ernst.

Krosius gave Ernst the passwords and the rendezvous point, and told him to put together a team of four men. 'Catch them, don't kill them,' he said. 'The Gestapo want them alive. Especially the American.'

'What if things get messy?' said Ernst. 'What if they put up a fight?'

'You'll be armed,' Krosius said. 'Won't you? Well, then.'

Ernst thought six men would be better than four. One of the six was Johann Nutzke, his sister's youngest. She had four children with four different men, none of whom had stayed around. Ernst wasn't surprised. She was a nag and a bitch.

Still, when she started whining about Johann, he told her it was her fault. 'You're a pushover. You're too soft on him. Let me have him for a while. I'll make a man out of him.' So Johann had come along. It was his fifteenth birthday.

The Gestapo were waiting along with Lieutenant Laumann and a dozen SS troops at the hunting cabin five hundred meters ahead. They had told Ernst not to waste any time.

'Let's go,' said Ernst. 'We've got to hurry.'

'Where to?' said Elke.

'Konstanz,' said Ernst, smiling, trying to seem friendly. He nodded to his men and started walking. Johann and one other man fell in with Ernst, while the other three waited for Elke, Charlie, and Fedor to move. But they didn't move.

A thousand marks was a big score for Ernst Nutzke. And to get hold of the money, he had to at least keep the pilot alive. When the three stayed where they were, Nutzke limped back. He tried to look friendly, but it didn't work. 'We've got to go if we're going to get you over the border. We don't have all day.'

Geranium, Clover, and Charlie all understood they had two choices: be questioned and tortured by the Gestapo, who they now knew would be waiting nearby, or make a run for it. Charlie said under his breath, 'We should run.' He looked at Clover and Geranium, and saw they understood. Three men were out in front of them and three behind. They couldn't shoot without hitting one another. It was just a meter to the ferns and then maybe five meters to the forest. 'On three, dive and crawl for the trees,' said Charlie. 'One . . .'

That was the moment young Johann decided to show Uncle Ernst what a big man he was. He ran up to Charlie, jammed his rifle up under Charlie's chin, and screamed, 'Get your stupid ass moving, godammit!' Charlie didn't understand the German, but he understood there was a loaded rifle there for the taking, and he took it. He grabbed Johann tight around the throat and moved sideways into the ferns. Johann struggled, but he was choking and couldn't do much. Clover and Geranium moved into the ferns with Charlie.

'Johann!' screamed Ernst. 'You goddamn idiot! You goddamn moron!' He was so angry he couldn't see straight. Ernst took the rifle off his shoulder and pointed it at Charlie, and the other four men did the same.

'God damn it! Let him go!' he screamed at Charlie. Charlie continued toward the trees. Then Ernst shot Johann. Then he shot Charlie. Then the other four opened up until Johann, Charlie, and Fedor were dead on the ground.

Beyond the Blue Horizon

When they fell, their bodies vanished into the tall ferns. And the five men had to search to make sure they were dead. They found Johann, then Charlie, then Fedor.

'Where's the other one?' said one of the men. 'The black?'

'Christ!' said Ernst. 'Find her!' The men started scurrying in circles through the ferns, looking everywhere. 'Find her!' screamed Ernst. He ran around frantically. 'Find her! Find her!' Ernst's men ran around in different directions.

The squad of SS men that had been waiting at the cabin came running with their guns ready. Laumann was close behind. 'Where's the pilot?' he shouted. But Ernst was hysterical, running in spite of his bad leg, stooped over, slashing at the ferns, searching, searching, searching, and finding nothing. Laumann tried to grab Ernst by the arm, but Ernst shook him off. So he slammed his Luger against Ernst's face and shouted again, 'Where's the goddamned pilot?'

Ernst limped over to where Charlie's body lay. 'Turn him over,' said Laumann. Ernst did as he was told. Charlie was dead. He was pretty shot up, but he was still recognizable.

'Who else is dead?'

Ernst showed him Fedor, then Johann.

'Jesus, this one's just a kid,' said Laumann. Ernst just looked at his own feet. He couldn't say that he had just killed his own nephew.

The men who had gone into the woods to find Elke came back. 'She's gone, Ernst. We can't find her.'

'What do you mean you can't find her? We've got to find her.' Without the black girl to give to the SS, Ernst had accomplished absolutely nothing. In fact, he had accomplished *less* than nothing. He had undermined an important operation to destroy a conspiracy against the Reich and he had killed a potentially important intelligence source. Ernst started searching through the ferns again.

Laumann turned away in disgust. 'Fritsche and Seligmann, go back to the cabin and get shovels,' he said.

'You!' he shouted at Ernst. 'You and your pals are going to bury these people.' Ernst had to explain finally that Johann was his nephew, and he had to take his body home. Johann, he explained, had been overwhelmed by the American. The American had killed the boy with his own weapon. Then Ernst and his friends had killed the American. They had no choice because he had Johann's gun. This was the story he would later tell his sister, adding, to calm her down, that Johann died protecting the Reich. His sister replied, 'I shit on your Reich. I shit on you, you stupid asshole.'

Fritsche and Seligmann came back with shovels, and Ernst and his four friends dug until Lieutenant Laumann told them it was deep enough. Laumann went through Fedor and Charlie's pockets, finding nothing. He took Charlie's dog tags from around his neck. He gave their rucksacks to Seligmann to take with them. Then Ernst and his friends dumped the bodies into the hole and filled it back up.

Ernst and his friends thought they would leave the way they had come. They had to take Johann home. But Laumann said nothing doing. They were coming with him back to the cabin, and from there back to Gestapo headquarters to be debriefed about the whole affair. And they would damn well bring Johann with them. Just to be sure there was no trouble, he ordered his men to collect their weapons. There were two shotguns, one hunting rifle, and three K-41 army rifles Krosius had provided to use for this operation.

At the cabin, Laumann ordered Ernst and his four friends into the back of one of the trucks where they were guarded by two SS men. Johann's body lay on the floor between their feet, wrapped in a canvas sheet. Ernst couldn't take his eyes off the red stain spreading slowly across the canvas.

They drove back to the Konstanz office of the Gestapo where they were grilled for three hours. After looking at it from every angle, the Gestapo man in charge concluded Ernst and his men were more stupid than criminal. That didn't mean that criminal charges would not be filed at some later time. But for now, they were free to go home.

* * *

Elke lay in the ferns. When Ernst had fired the first shot, she had dropped to the ground and scrambled like a crab, through ferns, through brambles, crashing into tree trunks, on and on through more ferns and more ferns. The ferns were endless. The shooting and screaming had seemed to go on forever. She lay as if in a dream. Her skin was torn from brambles, her body hurt everywhere. She didn't even know whether she had been shot.

Hours passed, and everyone was gone, and still she lay there. The moment played itself out again and again in her mind. She knew Charlie and Geranium were dead. She knew she had failed. She sobbed, sometimes in rage, sometimes in sorrow that she was alive, and sometimes in relief.

Night fell. She stood up. The rucksack was still on her back. She was maybe two hundred meters from the grave. She found her way back to it. She went down on her knees. She kissed her hand and touched the mound of earth into which Charlie and Fedor's bodies had been dumped. Then she sang softly. Grief makes us do strange things.

> Beyond the blue horizon
> Waits a beautiful day
> Goodbye to things that bore me
> Joy is waiting for me.
>
> I see a new horizon
> My life has only begun
> Beyond the blue horizon
> Lies a rising sun.

It was a warm night. Elke followed the path past the cabin, toward Schaffhausen and the border beyond. It took her two days walking and another three of watching and waiting for the right moment before she crossed into Switzerland.

Willi

Willi learned that the plan to get Charlie out of Germany had failed and the Flower Gang was compromised at about the same time Colonel Kurt Strang did. There was a phone call; Willi didn't recognize the voice. 'Bessingen has gone wrong,' a man said. 'We're compromised.' It could be a trick. But if it was a trick, they were still compromised. He thought he had no choice but to go.

Willi called Pierre. The woman answered. He warned her so that she could protect herself. He needed a car, he said. 'I'll pass it on,' she said. Then he called two others to say the network was compromised, which activated the chain. Each of them called two people and so on. The message always used exactly the same words: *Bessingen has gone wrong; we're compromised.*

Will called Bergemann and hung up when he answered. Bergemann called back a few minutes later from a safe phone.

Willi told Bergemann what he knew. 'I need details,' he said.

'I'll see what I can find out,' said Bergemann.

'I'm going south,' said Willi. 'I'll call you when I get there.'

Pierre was waiting at the appointed spot in a military ambulance. He was wearing a white coat.

'Why an ambulance?' Willi said.

'It was available, and it's fast,' said Pierre.

'And the white coat?'

'It's an ambulance,' said Pierre.

They headed directly for Bessingen.

They came to a roadblock performing routine stops. Pierre turned on the siren, and they waved him through. Lola and Willi were in the back. Lola had insisted on going along, and Willi couldn't say no. She was no longer safe at home.

As hard as it was to think about, Willi knew that they were probably too late to save Clover and the pilot. Fedor was not supposed to be with them, so Willi was not worried about Fedor. Still, he had to find out what was over and what could be saved, and he had to move quickly. At the same time, he was putting himself and others at risk by being out and about.

He had been a policeman long enough to understand that few criminal conspiracies remain secret for as long as theirs had. Just one small mistake – not even a mistake necessarily – could expose a loose thread. Then all a halfway decent detective – or, in this case, the Gestapo – had to do was tug on the thread, and the whole conspiracy would unravel and reveal itself. And now it had. It was a catastrophe.

Now the criminality being revealed was his, the conspiracy was his. He had been running a criminal organization. He had started it, had managed it, had enlarged it, had enlisted others – some were his friends, like Fedor, not to mention Lola, and some were entirely unknown to him – and now they were all at risk. Every one of them. He and they had managed a thousand different moving pieces, and eventually the inevitable had happened.

Willi wasn't frightened for himself. But he was frightened for all the others. He knew what would happen to them if they were caught. *When* they were caught. While you could think of contingencies and possibilities, you couldn't think of everything.

He had tried to prepare himself for this moment. But there was no way to prepare for the death and damage to so many lives. The best way to survive this moment was to start the next moment, to figure out what had happened, to save who could be saved, to salvage what could be salvaged, and to begin again.

Willi tried to imagine what had caused the unraveling, what had happened and who might be behind it. He was sure Werner Krosius figured in it somehow. Maybe he was just an informant. To Krosius, information was currency. But what information did he have, and where did he get it? There was no way to know that now, and too late for it to make any difference. He thought of finding Krosius, of killing him. But he was sure Krosius would have disappeared by now, and looking for him would be a waste of precious time.

Was there an actual traitor within the ranks, someone named after a flower? Willi didn't even know exactly how many people were in the network, much less who they all were. He didn't know who among them knew what. He wanted to weep. He pressed his hands into his eyes.

'What will we do when we get there?' said Lola.

Willi didn't know.

When they got to the abattoir, Geranium, Clover, and the American pilot were long gone. He knew they had been there; the blue yarn was gone. Willi told Pierre to drive to the rendez-vous point. They stopped at the stile. The blue yarn was gone there, too. There were recent tire tracks through the mud by the cabin, and some boot prints. That was a bad sign.

He walked backwards along the path until he got to the site of the massacre. What had happened was evident. All around, the tall ferns were torn up and trampled down. There were shell casings everywhere. Then he found the mound of freshly dug earth.

Willi stood there alone. Was this a grave? Whose was it? He feared that he knew, but he didn't know for sure. He thought he should dig it up and find out. But he couldn't bear to and went back to the ambulance.

'Let's go to the next checkpoint,' he said. Lola could see he was stricken.

The yarn was still knotted around the signpost six kilometers from the border and thirty kilometers north of Schaffhausen. 'Let's go to the border,' he said. You could hear the desperation in his voice.

'Stop, Willi,' said Lola. 'Don't. It's no use.' She was right, of course. She took his hand in both of hers.

It was a warm night. They sat by the signpost with the windows down. Pierre tried to see Willi in the rearview mirror, but all he could see was shadows. 'Where to?' he said.

'Riegsee,' said Willi after a long pause. 'The green house.'

Pierre started the engine and turned on the blackout headlamps. The faint beams filled with hundreds of fluttering moths, drawn by the light and blinded by it at the same time.

PART TWO

The Bulge

After the death of the American pilot, the SS and the Gestapo renewed their efforts to get Willi. They had new information from Joachim Ballitz and from Werner Krosius. They sent a dozen men to the Drehfelderstraße apartment. They pounded on the door until Adolf Jobst, the warden, came out from across the hall. He unlocked the door for them. They turned the place upside down but found nothing.

They asked Adolf a lot of questions about Herr and Frau Meier, and he told them everything he knew, which wasn't much. 'I think he used to be a policeman,' said Adolf.

They already knew that. 'Why do you have his keys?' they said.

'They had a cat. I took care of it sometimes.'

'Where's the cat now?'

'I don't know. It got out after the last bombing and never came back.'

They asked him about Elke Oldenburg.

'I don't know her,' he said.

The SS said if they learned Adolf had held anything back, anything at all, they would come for him.

'I've told you everything I know,' he said.

After the green house, Pierre had taken Lola to the Swiss border, and she had gone across with false papers. She was staying with a cousin in Zürich, so she was safe. Elke was in Zürich at the same time, but neither one knew the other was there.

Willi was in Germany, deep in the Bavarian Forest. Eberhardt von Hohenstein had offered Willi a woodcutter's hut, one of several scattered across the von Hohenstein estate and surrounded by vast forest. The hut was four kilometers from the manor house, down a grassy double track that led nowhere else. The hut was furnished with a cast-iron cooking stove and a few sticks of furniture. There was a crank-powered radio, too. Willi strung up a wire antenna to listen to the news from the BBC.

The suffering and deaths of the pilot and Fedor and Elke – he did not know which – were never far from his mind. He mulled over ways he might find their killers if he survived the war.

Eberhardt took provisions to Willi, by car or on horseback. The two friends sat outside in all but the worst weather. Eberhardt marveled at the stack of wood Willi had cut and split – thirty cubic meters, at least.

The days were getting shorter. Sometimes when the wind blew, acorns rained down, sounding like gunshots on the metal roof.

Eberhardt said he thought there was a family of owls living nearby. Snowy owls, said Willi. He had seen one of the parents.

They discussed what they were reading – Willi read Schiller's plays, which Eberhardt had brought him in a ten-volume leather-bound edition. Eberhardt was reading Shakespeare at Willi's recommendation. The conversation always turned to the news eventually, the relentless offensives of the summer that had brought the Russians to Germany's doorstep. And the catastrophic Operation Walküre.

Walküre was a plot to first assassinate Hitler and then take over the government. Both Eberhardt and Willi knew of the plot from several of the plotters, mostly military officers. Many of the plotters knew each other, which was dangerous. But it had to be that way, said Willi. It was a desperate plan, said Eberhardt. Desperate plans were what you did when there was nothing left to lose.

Walküre came apart spectacularly on July 20 when the assassination failed. The conspirators scrambled to escape or to disavow their part in the conspiracy. Some tried to denounce their fellow conspirators. Hitler, driven mad by the betrayal, rounded up people by the thousands.

Willi's friend and mentor Benno Horvath was arrested in a hotel in Berlin. Margarete, back in Munich, never saw or heard from him again. Like many others, Benno had a quick trial in front of Roland Freisler, the President of the People's Court. Freisler screamed and shouted abuse and then sentenced him to death. Benno was hanged from a wire noose along with countless others. The hangings were filmed, and the films were shown to soldiers, officials, and the public. It was meant as a warning, but most refused to watch. They just covered their eyes or looked away.

Despite Hitler's insane pronouncements of imminent victory, the Third Reich was running on terror and oppression at home, and hopeless schemes on the battlefield. The Allies had eventually pushed their way out of Normandy, and by late August they were in Paris. Charles de Gaulle marched Free French forces down the Champs-Élysées. Willi listened to the cheering crowds on the radio.

When the Allies reached the Ardennes, their advance stalled. They had got ahead of their supply convoys and had to wait while they caught up. They weren't worried. The depleted German army was drafting fifteen-year-old boys and old men by then. But Hitler believed (and which of his generals dared contradict him?) that a massive counter-offensive would split the Americans and Brits in two, and he could finish them off. Then he would turn his attention to the Russians, who were bogged down in Poland, and finish *them* off.

On December 16, four Panzer armies consisting of more than five hundred tanks and four hundred thousand soldiers attacked the Americans in the Ardennes Forest, where the terrain was difficult and their line was weak. The Allies were pushed back, stretching Allied defenses thinner still. Blizzards and freezing rain covered everything in layers of ice and snow. Temperatures dropped to twenty below zero. Tanks froze to the ground overnight and had to be pried loose in the morning. But the bulge in the line held long enough for the Allies to bring up reinforcements. After six gruesome weeks, they drove the Germans back.

One sunny February day, Eberhardt rode out to see Willi. He tied the horse to the woodpile, stamped on the stone doorstep to get the snow off his boots, and came inside. He stood with his back to the hot stove. 'Something has happened,' said Eberhardt. 'You remember Erich Lobe?'

'Schloß Barzelhof,' said Willi. 'Yes, I remember.' Schloß Barzelhof was the boarding school they had all attended.

'He's Gestapo and an SS colonel now; normally, he's in Frankfurt. But he's in Passau with a big detachment of SS and Gestapo. They've set up in city hall. I just saw him there.'

'You saw him? Why?'

'I was summoned.'

'Does he know where you live?'

'Yes. He came home with me from Barzelhof one Christmas.'

'Why is he in Passau?'

'He says he's hunting "leftover" Walküre conspirators. A new initiative. He asked me about you. He wondered whether you were involved with Walküre in some way.'

'Had he heard that I was?'

'No, I don't think so. But he knew about the American pilot. I couldn't make out what or how much he knew.'

'What did you tell him?'

'I said that I hadn't seen you since we left Barzelhof over thirty years ago.'

'Did he believe you?'

'He said he did, but I doubt it. You know Erich. He loved the cat-and mouse stuff.'

'Do you think he'll come see you out here?'

'I don't think so. But we have to be ready if he does.'

Most nights, Willi couldn't sleep. He wasn't afraid, but he felt helpless, paralyzed. On moonlit nights, he walked through the woods. He watched for the owls but never saw one again. He made elaborate and completely unworkable plans. He needed to do something, take some kind of action, *any* action against the Reich, against Hitler, against Erich Lobe, against Werner Krosius. Lying on his cot in the dark, his eyes wide open, he studied the architecture of imaginary bridges and planned how to blow them up.

Lola was not there to damp down his wild visions. Willi had not communicated with her or she with him since July. Over seven months. All he could do now was imagine her in her cousin's apartment. Will had been there once before the war. It was a nice apartment with a view of the lake. But who knew where she really was, what had happened once she was over the border? Who knew *anything*?

What had their life been like? How had they spent evenings? Normal evenings, that is. Had they even had normal evenings? He tried to summon the taste of her goulash but couldn't. Her voice had begun disappearing from his mind. Her face was becoming indistinct in his recollection. He would, of course, recognize her when he finally saw her again. But when he tried to construct her features in his mind's eye, he couldn't quite manage it. Did it really happen that quickly, or was something wrong with him? What color were her eyes? What were her hands like? They were strong square hands, the hands of someone who worked. Her hair was red. He still knew that.

On March 9, 1944, the day he heard the Americans had crossed the Rhine, Willi announced to Eberhardt that he wanted to go to Passau.

'There's nothing you can do in Passau, Willi, except maybe fall into Gestapo hands.'

Willi told him about Werner Krosius and his connection to the catastrophe that haunted him. He was sure Krosius had brought about the deaths in the forest. Krosius would be impossible to find once the Reich collapsed. 'I need to start looking before it's too late. A few questions, that's all, and then we'll come right back. Will you take me?'

'No,' said Eberhardt. 'Definitely not.'

'Then I'll go on my own.'

Eberhardt knew Willi well enough to know he would find a way to get there on his own, even if it meant stealing Eberhardt's car. And Willi was the worst driver Eberhardt had even seen. He drove as if brakes were for other people. So Eberhardt drove him.

The Woodcutters

Willi wanted to go during a blizzard. Nobody would be out and about, and so there probably wouldn't be any checkpoints either. He got his wish two days later. They had loaded Eberhardt's old Opel Blitz with firewood. The truck was good in the snow, and the load would help with traction. And if they were asked, they were woodcutters delivering wood.

The snow swirled and blew from every angle. The wipers were useless, and the windshield was soon coated with ice outside and in. Willi tried to wipe it clear with his hands, but it was a losing battle.

A trip that should have taken an hour took three. Late in the morning, they crossed the river and pulled up in front of Donau Fixtures. Eberhardt kept the engine running, and Willi got out.

The shop was closed, but there was a light on inside. Willi knocked. No one answered, so he knocked louder, again and again. He was about to go down the alley to look for a rear entrance when he saw someone come out of a back room. A man unlocked the door and opened it a crack. As he did, a gust of wind blew a cloud of snow at him, and he had to fight to keep the door from flying open.

'We're closed,' he said through the crack.

'I know,' said Willi. 'We've got a load of firewood here. Where do you want it?'

'What?'

'A firewood delivery,' said Willi and pointed at the truck.

The man was confused. After a moment's thought, he said, 'Step inside.' He pushed the door shut with Willi's help. 'Firewood?' he said. 'I don't understand.'

'Is Herr Krosius here? He's the one that ordered it.'

'What? Krosius? That can't be,' said the man. 'There's been a mistake.'

'What do you mean?' said Willi.

'Werner Krosius?' said the man.

'That's him. He called in an order.'

'That can't be,' said the man again. 'Werner Krosius is dead.'

'What?' said Willi. 'Are you sure?'

'Yes, I'm sure,' said the man.

'Did he just die? Because the order was called in last Friday.'

'No. It was over a month ago. February the first, I think. His building was bombed. A direct hit.'

'Well, somebody's having their way with him now. How'd you find out he was dead?'

'Two policemen. They came the day after the air raid, two of them, and said he wouldn't be in because he was dead. I thought it was odd at the time. I didn't know the police ever did that – tell you somebody was dead.'

'Where'd he live?' said Willi. 'Do you know the address?'

'Sure. Prinzregentenstraße, number nine. I went myself to have a look. The building took a direct hit. There was nothing left but rubble.'

'Somebody's played a joke on us,' said Willi, pointing toward the truck again.

'I guess so,' said the man. 'I'm sorry. For what it's worth, Krosius was the best accountant I've ever had.'

'Is that so?' said Willi. 'Are you the owner?'

'Yes. Werner was a really good employee. The best accountant ever.'

'What did you know about him?' said Willi.

'Not much. He was a very private guy.'

'Did he work for you every day?'

'Well, he took time off. A good bit of time off. But he always did his work.'

'Did you know about his black-market activity?'

'What? No,' said the owner. 'Black market? Say . . . who are you, anyway?'

Willi pulled out his old police badge and flashed it in front of the owner. 'Did you know about his involvement in the black market?'

'Was he really? I mean, no, I didn't know a thing. I swear. I wouldn't have stood for that.'

'Do you still have his books?'

'Of course,' said the owner. He didn't want any trouble. He took Willi back to Krosius's office and showed him the company ledgers. They were neat and meticulous, each column filled with carefully written names of plumbing suppliers, supplies, and numbers.

Willi looked around the office. The shelves were completely empty. All the desk drawers were empty. There was a new blotter on top of the desk. A new desk calendar as well.

'Did you change the blotter or the calendar?'

'No. Werner must have done that.'

'And you didn't clean out the office.'

'No. This is how he left it.'

'And then he died?'

The owner shrugged. Willi thanked the man and left.

The snow had let up. 'What did you learn?' said Eberhardt as they drove off.

'Krosius wants us to think he's dead.'

'But he's not?'

'I'd be surprised if he is. He planned his exit in advance. Nothing, and I mean *nothing*, was left in his office.

'Let's drive down Prinzregentenstraße,' said Willi. They did. The building at number nine was gone.

Peace

Millions of people were wandering the German countryside: soldiers left on the battlefield, others that had surrendered in droves, prisoners freed from camps, and ordinary people, damaged and homeless, searching for what no longer existed. Hitler was dead; Germany had surrendered. The victorious Allies and their new German partners now had to create peace and order out of chaos and ruin.

The Allies divided Germany into four zones. Munich was in the American zone. A small detachment of American military police moved into the ruined police headquarters and set about reconstituting the Munich police department, 'denazifying' it as best they could. That wasn't going to be easy, since so many police had been enthusiastic National Socialist Party members. But, as Major Becker, the American MP in charge, said, 'Those are the cards we've been dealt.'

The Americans installed Walther Breuer as a new chief of detectives in the fifth precinct. They set about putting together a new police force, rehiring former policemen, including Willi Geismeier as a detective.

Police Captain Breuer looked over Willi's record from his earlier time as a policeman. Then he looked Willi up and down. Willi was thin, and his clothes were tattered and a little loose on him. His face was brown from the sun. His close-cropped hair was turning white.

'You used to be a good detective,' said Breuer. Willi knew what was coming. A remark like that was always followed by 'but' and then a list of his shortcomings: that he never followed police protocol, that he never followed orders, that he wasn't a team player.

Those had been the complaints before Hitler, during Hitler, and now in American Occupied Germany, there they were again. The new protocols negotiated between the American Major Becker and the newly installed Munich police officials were meant to promote good policing, while at the same time protecting these old Nazis, largely chiefs and captains like Captain Wilhelm Breuer, a former SS major who had served in various camps, including Dachau. You needed these guys, Becker explained to his men, because they were the ones who knew how a police department worked.

Breuer was mad. Willi had just refused a transfer to police headquarters. 'Damn it, Geismeier, what's wrong with you? *It's a promotion!*' Willi would be chief of national operations. It was a new position, Breuer said. He said it would take advantage of Willi's proven skills.

'What's wrong with that?' said Bergemann when Willi told him. Bergemann was in a different precinct. He didn't remember Breuer.

'What "particular skills"?' said Willi. 'It's a made-up job. There aren't any "national operations." They're "promoting" me into a dead-end job to get me out of the way.'

Right after Willi had rejoined the force, he had caught what looked to Breuer at least like an open-and-shut case. The police had arrested a thief for murdering a pawnbroker. The pawnbroker had been found on the floor behind the counter, shot through the head. 'It looks like a robbery gone wrong,' said Breuer. 'We want to tie this one up quickly.' Breuer wanted to impress the Americans. But it wasn't immediately apparent that anything had been taken, and to Willi, the gunshot wound looked more like an execution than the quick shot of a scared robber.

On searching the pawnshop, Willi found a pocket calendar in the dead man's jacket with indecipherable notations:

M 440 – Hansi K.
Z 446 – Bobi.
M 520 – Gerd.
H 444 – Gretl.

Rolf Fasan, the man the police had arrested, was a veteran of both wars. Rolf said he had come to the shop to pawn a ring. Seeing the owner dead on the floor, he had run away. When Willi asked to see the ring, Rolf said he had lost it.

A woman had had her purse snatched the day before the

murder. She had been taking *her* mother's jewelry, including a diamond ring, to be repaired. Willi suspected Rolf had snatched the purse, but he didn't think Rolf had shot the pawnbroker. The nature of the wound and the coded calendar suggested that Rolf might have stumbled into something bigger than he could handle. 'Where'd you get the ring, Rolf?' he said.

'It was my mother's,' said Rolf.

'And you stole it from her?' said Willi.

'She gave it to me,' said Rolf, trying his best to look indignant. He didn't quite pull it off. 'I'm her only son,' he added.

'And now you've lost it.'

'Yeah,' said Fasan.

'If I search your room, Rolf, what other gifts from your mother am I going to find? A French watch, maybe? A gold and sapphire bracelet? A woman's embroidered purse?'

'I found it, Detective, I swear.'

'You're lying, Rolf. But I don't think you killed the pawnbroker. We'll get back to your purse-snatching in a bit. What interests me now is why you picked that particular pawnshop, since there are other pawnshops closer to home. Have you fenced stuff with him before?'

'I don't know what you're talking about, Detective.'

Willi studied his own hands. He closed and opened his fists. Rolf wondered whether Willi was going to hit him.

'Listen to me, Rolf,' said Willi after a long silence. 'I can make an airtight case against you for this murder. In fact, that's what my captain wants me to do. You went in there to rob him; he wouldn't give you the money, so you shot him. Witnesses saw you go in and come out. You're a thief. He's dead. You're the killer. Airtight. Or' – he flexed his hands again – 'or you can help me find out what this murder is *really* all about.'

'They'll kill me,' said Rolf.

'Who?' said Willi.

'I used Gerhard as a fence before. That's why I went there. To fence the lady's jewels. I used him before. He gave me a fair price. If I had known . . .' Rolf stopped to think how to go on. 'I saw a guy on the street. I didn't see him come out of the shop, but I know he was there. I know who he is. And he knows who I am. He saw me. They'll kill me.' He buried his face in his hands.

Willi pushed the calendar across the table and pointed to an entry. 'What's this mean, Rolf?'

'I don't know. What is it?'

'A pocket diary. It was in Gerhard's pocket.' Willi pointed to the entry again.

Rolf studied it. He looked at other entries. Then closed the diary and looked up at Willi with fear in his eyes. He couldn't stop shaking his head.

'What is it, Rolf?'

'Hotel rooms,' he said.

'Hotel rooms?'

'Z for Zentral, M for Münchener.'

'And the names?' said Willi. 'Who are the names, Rolf?'

Rolf couldn't make himself say it, so Willi did. 'Children? Are they children, Rolf?'

Rolf just nodded.

Bernie Pautsch

The man Rolf Fasan had seen on the street after leaving the pawnshop was named Bernie Pautsch. And Rolf was right: Bernie had recognized him. Bernie had never been a Nazi, but that was his only virtue. He had briefly been a policeman, just long enough to realize that criminality was more lucrative outside the police department than in it. He did some armed robbery and served two years in Dachau in the early thirties when Dachau was still just a prison camp.

After Dachau, Bernie went looking for something less risky than robbery. He got involved in smuggling, in the black market, in drug dealing, and eventually in prostitution, particularly the prostitution of children. He had been surprised to find out there were a lot of people, many in high places, with an appetite for children as sexual toys. While Bernie thought sex with children was weird, he saw it as an opportunity to make lots of money. Germany had a lot of parentless children on the streets, willing to do just about anything to survive. And highly placed clients – businessmen and Nazi officials in the old days, businessmen and civil servants now – would protect him from prosecution, since if he went down, they were going with him. It was, he thought, a win-win situation.

The trouble was, it was a complicated business and there were too many ways it could go wrong. For one thing, the children had to be controlled – kept happy or intimidated, as the case might be. Then there were the meeting places. A few clients wanted the children to come to their homes, but most wanted to meet someplace else, someplace anonymous, preferably a hotel. Munich didn't yet have many functioning hotels, and they were mostly booked up for visiting American officials. And finding a hotel willing to play along was also tricky.

So far, Willi had figured out that Bernie did the recruitment of children. Gerhard the dead pawnbroker, he figured, had been in charge of the money – payments to the hotel, payments to the pimps, and bribes and payoffs. And Gerhard had been skimming some for himself. Willi thought Bernie had gone to the pawnshop to confront Gerhard about it. Bernie knew Gerhard had a gun – all pawnbrokers did, so when Gerhard pulled out the gun, Bernie took it from him, knocked him to floor and shot him between the eyes.

Willi reported all this to Captain Breuer who listened with a mixture of astonishment and dread. This was exactly the kind of mess you could expect when Geismeier got involved in a case. 'So why haven't you arrested this Pautsch character?' he said.

'I need more evidence,' said Willi. 'I don't have enough to hold him. Plus, I'm pretty sure we're dealing with a big enterprise here, Captain. There's not just the trafficking of children. There's prostitution, there's drugs, there's financial fraud – money laundering, et cetera. It takes more than one guy to run an operation like this. There have to be lots of people involved. I'll follow Pautsch and see where he takes us.'

Captain Breuer was not a client of Pautsch's sex ring, but still he dreaded reporting any of this to police headquarters. Not because he knew who would be implicated, but because he didn't. This was the kind of investigation that could explode in unexpected quarters, and with Geismeier doing the investigating in his bull-in-a-china-shop way, you never knew where it was going to blow up and who was going to blow up with it.

Breuer's superior, the Munich chief of detectives, was a man named Gleiwitz. He had been a policeman as long as Willi had. He had long admired Willi's police work and had more than once defended him when he had got into trouble. 'I'm inclined to give Geismeier free rein,' he said. 'Yes, he's a bull in a china shop, but he tends to get results, Breuer. Let's let him do his work his way.'

There was not much Breuer could do to stop Willi. But he could warn department colleagues about the coming upheaval. The warning filtered up and down through the ranks. The following week, there were three unexpected resignations from the police department, two from vice and one from headquarters. Willi got wind of Breuer's warnings, and he added the names of the three resignations to the list of people he wanted to interview.

Lola

Willi stood up as Lola came through the door. She was wearing the green dress he liked so much. Her hair was showing little wisps of white at the temples. She looked around the room, spotted him, and threaded her way between the tables to where he stood.

'Willi,' she said.

He reached out with both hands and held her arms. She reached out, too. It was awkward with the table in their way, not quite an embrace. There were lines around her eyes that he hadn't seen before. They had each been back in Munich a while.

It hadn't been easy to find each other, and neither one had been impatient to do so. Lola's father was dead, and her mother had gone to live with a younger sister in Augsburg. For a while, Lola thought of living in Augsburg, too. Finally, when she was ready, she found Bergemann, and he found Willi, and now here they were.

Finding each other again was only the first step. There was still that awful, terrifying year to get past – the war, the end of the war, not knowing if the other was dead or alive.

'How are you?' she said.

'Fine,' he said. 'I'm glad to see you,' he added. He lowered his eyes. It wasn't the kind of thing he said very easily, especially in a busy public place. They were in a neighborhood *Gasthaus* near where she was living.

'Let's sit,' she said. They sat down and Willi immediately jumped up. He had sat on the bouquet of flowers. He handed them across the table and a few petals fell on to the tablecloth. She laughed. Then he laughed.

'How long have you been in Munich?' Willi said.

'A month,' said Lola. 'When I came back, I needed to be alone.'

'Me, too,' said Willi. 'I didn't look for you right away.'

'It's fine,' said Lola.

Lola had found a place to stay with an old friend of her mother. The woman let her use a basement apartment in exchange for a little housecleaning. 'It doesn't amount to much work. I think she mainly wants the company, someone else in the house at night.'

After a few days in Munich, Lola had gone to the Hotel zur Kaiserkrone where she had once managed the Mahogany Room bar. The hotel was a ruin. Most of the roof was gone, the walls were buttressed by large timbers, the windows were out. But somehow the Mahogany Room was intact.

Herr Kuzinski, who had managed the hotel, was now running the bar. His face lit up when Lola came in. He and Lola embraced joyfully. 'Wait and see,' he said. 'The hotel will be back. The owners have already asked me to be manager,' he said. Lola looked around doubtfully.

As unlikely as it seemed, within the year, reconstruction began on the hotel. And a year later it reopened with great ceremony as the Grand Hotel zur Kaiserkrone. Herr Kuzinski was made the manager once again, presiding over the large staff, making sure everything was just as it should be. But for now, all that seemed like an impossible dream.

Willi and Lola ordered supper. There was not much on the menu. She had a mushroom omelet and a green salad, and Willi had a sausage, sauerkraut, and boiled potatoes. They drank beer. She asked Willi how it was, being back at the police department. Strange, he said. The people who had wanted him dead were still there. Gruber was somewhere; Willi had yet to find out where.

Bergemann had to guide him, he said, had to tell him who to watch out for and who could be trusted.

'That sounds hard,' said Lola. 'Are you going to stay?'

'For now,' said Willi. 'There's still that unfinished business.'

Lola cocked her head and raised her eyebrows.

'Fedor, Elke Oldenburg, and the pilot.'

'I know what you meant. Isn't that over?'

'Not for me,' said Willi. 'I need to find out what happened, what went wrong, and who did it.'

'And when you do?'

'I don't know yet. Justice maybe?'

Lola looked at the flowers he had brought. 'You think I should let it go, don't you?' said Willi.

'I wish you could,' she said. 'But I know you can't. Once a cop, always a cop.'

'The fact that the war is over and lost changes many things, but it doesn't change everything,' said Willi. 'You know about the trials in Nürnberg?'

'Of course,' she said. 'This isn't the same.'

'No,' said Willi. 'I know that.'

'It's not even really about justice, is it?' she said.

'It is, I think. But only partly. Revenge, too, if I'm honest.' Willi tried to sort through his feelings, but they were so tangled that they defied explanation. He ended by saying, 'I can't explain it. It's just something that's in me, that's all.' In fact, that *was* the explanation.

Lola reached across the table and touched his hand. 'I know,' she said.

'Herr Kuzinski offered me a bartending job,' she said.

'You took it, I hope?'

'I did. He's running the bar now, so bartending was all he could offer. But I need to work. Remember how the bar was full of SS back then? Now it's full of Americans.'

'Maybe when the hotel comes back, he'll give you the bar to run again.'

'He said he would,' said Lola.

'That's great,' said Willi. 'I know you loved that job.'

Willi went home with Lola, and they spent the night in each other's arms, the first time in over a year. The next morning Lola made coffee – real coffee – and grilled toast in the oven. She had butter in her small refrigerator and wonderfully bitter marmalade. They sat at the table and ate. The sun sent pale rays through a window high in the basement wall. Neither one of them could think of a single thing that was missing. And yet there was that new space between them.

Elke

Thanks to a musician friend, Elke Oldenburg had found work in Zürich as an attendant at the public baths. She gave out towels by the pool, watched the lockers, and swept and mopped up at the end of the day. The pay was meager, but it was just enough to afford a quarter share of an apartment with her friend Ilse and two other women.

Old Herr Luthi the night watchman let her swim after they had closed for the day and everyone else had left. He watched her secretly from behind a door. She knew he did it, but he was an old man, and she guessed it was one of the few pleasures in his life, so she let it go.

The pool was surrounded and lit by sconces. When Elke first dived in, shards of golden light danced across the walls and the low ceiling. Floating on her back, she had the feeling she was breathing through gills, like a mermaid. In moments like that, Herr Luthi understood what beautiful meant, and Elke could almost forget about Geranium and Charlie Herder.

Elke was haunted by what had happened. She blamed herself for their deaths. She should have seen the signs, she told herself, although there had been no signs. Once, she took a train to Schaffhausen and found her way back into Germany. She retraced their steps from the abattoir to the Frauenberg Hunting Club and back again, looking for useful clues, but, of course, finding none. The grave was overgrown with ferns, but she found it. There were still a few shell casings around. The cabin had been broken into and was filled with trash and old bottles.

Sometimes she prowled along the border, looking at the guards through binoculars, thinking for some reason that the killer they had called Ernst might be a border guard. But if he was, she never saw him. She looked in cemeteries in Konstanz for the grave of the boy called Johann, but without his last name it was impossible.

With the end of the war, nothing much changed for her, until one day in October. She was at the train station and looked up at the schedule board of departures. She saw trains listed for Paris, Milan, Geneva, Cologne, Hamburg, Berlin. She could be in Munich in twelve hours with changes in Friedrichshafen and Ulm.

She bought a third-class ticket. She had a window seat. There were no SS patrolling through the cars, no identification checks. No one was taken off the train. Just a conductor walking through punching tickets. The only soldiers were Americans, and they were passengers. They all looked like some version of Charlie. Once, they caught her looking, and she looked away.

In Munich, she took a streetcar to Drehfelderstraße. The buildings were still a mess, but the rubble had been removed from the streets and there was construction everywhere. Number 120 looked pretty much as it always had, except there was a long crack running up the facade.

When she knocked on the door on the fifth floor, Adolf answered. It took a second, but then he threw his arms around her, which surprised them both. 'Frieda!' he called. Frieda came from the other room and embraced her, too. They invited her to stay and have supper. They had been getting packages of food from American relatives they didn't even know they had.

Elke didn't want to talk about the last year, and neither did Adolf or Frieda. She asked about Herr and Frau Meier. Were they still here?

'No,' said Adolf. 'His real name is Willi Geismeier.'

'Is Herr Geismeier a policeman?' said Elke.

'Yes,' said Adolf. 'A detective. How did you know?'

'I guessed,' said Elke. 'What's he like?'

Adolf knew that Willi was in the fifth precinct, but he didn't know much more than that. 'Go see him,' said Adolf. 'I think he thinks you're dead.'

The next morning, as Willi approached the precinct house, he saw Elke waiting in a doorway across the street. He broke into a trot, and when he reached her, he took her hand in both of his and smiled. 'I'm so glad to see you,' he said.

'Did you think I was dead?' she said.

'I didn't think so, but I didn't know for sure.'

'Geranium and the pilot,' she said.

'Yes, I know,' he said.

She studied him for a moment.

'What is it?' he said.

'In a way, it's as though we're different people now, isn't it?' she said. 'There's then and there's now.'

People going into the building looked at them, especially at Elke. She was as beautiful as ever, and she was black, so you never knew why they were looking.

'Come inside,' said Willi.

'No,' said Elke. 'Can we meet later?'

'Pick me up at noon.'

'OK,' she said. Then: 'No, let's meet somewhere else.'

'The East Cemetery?' said Willi.

'Yes,' said Elke.

In the East Cemetery, they sat on a bench under a chestnut tree. The tree's leaves had turned yellow, and the ground around them was strewn with chestnuts.

'I had many meetings here during the war,' said Willi. He leaned over and picked up a chestnut. He peeled off its spiny shell, and the brown nut gleamed in his palm. 'Tell me everything,' he said.

Elke started with the confrontations with Charlie while they were on the *Alm*. 'I don't think he had ever talked to a black person before.'

'No,' said Willi. 'You're probably right.'

'But he learned to,' she said.

'I'm glad to hear that,' said Willi.

'Yes,' said Elke. She smiled, remembering something.

Then she described the hike down to the Zoellners', the ride in the cattle truck, the roadblock, the slaughterhouse, the night at the abattoir, the walk to the Frauenberg Hunting Club, the blue yarn.

Then the killing. She remembered every moment of that, and it came out in a torrent of words. She remembered hearing the names Ernst and Johann. They were related, she thought – father and son maybe. She thought they were from Konstanz. Something told her Ernst might be a border guard. Johann had attacked Charlie, and Charlie took his rifle away. Ernst killed Johann so he could kill Charlie and Geranium.

'What made you think Ernst was a border guard?' said Willi.

'It was just a guess,' she said. 'Or maybe I saw him when I used to cross the border. I don't know. What was Geranium's name?'

'Fedor Blaskowitz,' said Willi.

'Fedor Blaskowitz,' said Elke. She said it again. 'The SS made Ernst and the others bury them where they fell. They're still there. I put stones on the grave later. The SS arrested the killers and took them away. The SS were mad, I guess, because they had wanted us alive, to interrogate us.'

Elke described searching along the border for the man called Ernst, then going back to the abattoir, and then to the cabin looking for clues. She didn't mention searching the cemeteries for Johann. That seemed crazy to her now. 'I want to find Ernst. And the others,' she said.

'I know,' said Willi. But then he said that although it had been cold-blooded and premeditated murder, it would now be defended in court, if it ever came to trial, as an act of war. A halfway decent defense lawyer would argue that the killing had occurred between combatants, which was what happened in war. There were literally millions of such acts during the war, and very few would ever be prosecuted. To find the perpetrators wouldn't be all that difficult, he said, but to charge and prosecute them would be.

'So you're not going to try?' said Elke.

'I didn't say that,' said Willi. 'I will try. And while Ernst and his men did the killing, there are others that sent them to do it. Someone hired them, told them you were coming, and maybe even paid them to kill you. Someone betrayed you and us. I want to find them as well.'

'Do you have any ideas?' said Elke.

'I do,' said Willi. 'But none I can share.'

Helmut Raeder

Willi had an appointment with former Sergeant Helmut Raeder, a long-time member of the Munich vice squad. Raeder was one of the three police officers that had resigned after Breuer's warning about child prostitution had filtered through the department. Willi gave no indication what the interview might be about. 'A case you were on,' said Willi. 'Can we meet?'

'Absolutely,' Raeder had said. 'Absolutely.'

Raeder had worried the pawnbroker's murder might uncover the child prostitution business and had quickly resigned, hoping his resignation would take him out of the picture. Willi Geismeier had said he was a detective from the fifth precinct, and Raeder remembered that was Hermann Gruber's old precinct. They had been friends back before Gruber had gone full Nazi. Gruber was up in Nürnberg now after leaving the Munich police in a hurry right after the war.

Raeder gave Gruber a call and they chatted about old times. Then Raeder said, 'Did you know a guy named Willi Geismeier back in the day?'

Hermann felt the hair on the back of his neck stand up. 'Why?' he said.

'We're supposed to meet tomorrow morning,' said Raeder.

'What's he want?' said Gruber.

'He said he wants to ask me about a case,' he said.

'What case?' said Gruber.

'He didn't say,' said Raeder.

'You didn't ask?' said Gruber.

'I did, but he didn't say.'

'Well, whatever you do, don't tell him you know me. That son of a bitch is nothing but trouble.'

'Why, what's he to you?'

'I was his old sergeant. That asshole ruined my career.'

* * *

The café where Willi and Helmut met had put a few tables out on the sidewalk. It was a warm, sunny day. If you looked into the park from where they sat, you could forget for a moment that you were surrounded by rubble. Helmut ordered a beer; Willi had tea.

Willi asked Helmut a few questions about a recent case Helmut had worked on for most of a year. The case, illegal gambling, had been tough to make, but eventually Helmut had busted it wide open. The two operators of a traveling casino had been convicted and given three years each, and Helmut and his squad had gotten commendations. 'And it was just the two men?' Willi said. 'You'd think it would take more than the two of them.'

'I know,' said Helmut, 'but it was just the two guys. They tried to put it off on others, but they all had alibis.'

Willi turned the page in his notebook. 'Who is Bobi?' he said.

'What?' said Helmut. He almost knocked over his beer.

'Bo-bi,' said Willi, enunciating carefully as though Helmut hadn't heard. 'Who is Bobi?'

Helmut stared at Willi, his eyes a little too steady. Finally, he said, 'I don't know any Bobi.'

'I see,' said Willi. 'Does the Hotel Zentral mean anything to you?'

'It's a hotel on the Bahnhofplatz. Other than that, no, it doesn't.'

'You've never been there?'

'No.'

'Really? The night clerk – I should say *former* night clerk – says he's checked you in.'

'No. He's wrong. I've never been inside the place.'

'He says you come by for an hour or so on various nights, most recently Sunday, a week ago. Nine thirty. Would you like other dates and room numbers?' Willi read them from his notebook. 'The clerk was quite specific. He's in jail, by the way, charged with human trafficking, procurement, and other crimes. He knew your name and your rank, even though you used a false name. And he knows Bobi's name and could give a very detailed and accurate description of you both. Bobi, he said, is about eleven or twelve, but small for his age. Dark hair, blue eyes. He said Bobi always arrives after you do. He was usually brought by a minder, a man who waited while Bobi went upstairs. Does that jog your memory?'

Helmut got up from his chair, put fifty pfennigs on the table to pay for his beer. 'I think we're done here,' he said.

'If you walk away now, Raeder, things will go a lot worse for you than if you stay and answer some questions. Your sexual perversions are disgusting. But frankly, I'm more interested in the traffickers and pimps than I am in you.'

Raeder thought for a moment, then sat back down. 'What do you want to know?' he said.

Willi asked him about Bernie Pautsch. He didn't know who that was. He didn't know who Gerhard the dead pawnbroker was either. Until Breuer had warned him, he hadn't known the murder of the pawnbroker was connected. 'My only contact was Emil. The night clerk.'

'Who brought the boy to your room?'

'I don't know. I never saw him.'

'Never? Did you ever talk to him?'

'No. Never. He waited downstairs while the boy went up. I never even heard his voice.'

'How did you set up a date?'

'I had a phone number. I called and said I wanted a date. I left my name and number.'

'A date?'

'That's what I was told to say.'

'What name did you use?'

'Meier.'

Willi laughed.

'That's funny?' said Raeder.

'It's just that I used that name myself once. And what's the number?'

Raeder knew it by heart.

'Who did you talk to?'

'I don't know.'

'So, did you talk to the boy when you were together or just . . .'

'No, we didn't talk that much,' said Helmut. He put his head in his hands. 'Are you enjoying this?'

'When you talked, what did you talk about?' said Willi.

'He likes football,' said Helmut. 'I told him I'd get tickets. I said I'd take him to a match. And I would have too . . .'

Bobi

Willi called the number Helmut had given him. A man answered and took Willi's information. Willi heard street noise in the background and some sort of public announcement. 'Who is this?' said Willi. 'Where are you?'

'Someone will call you back,' said the man and hung up.

Someone called back. Willi gave a name; the man gave him a time, said what the charge would be and how to pay.

Willi checked in at the Zentral as instructed. Lola was with him. The new night clerk had Willi register and gave him the room key. Lola had thought Willi was crazy when he explained what he was doing, and even crazier when he asked her to come along.

'Absolutely not,' she said. 'How could you even ask?'

'It's for the boy,' said Willi. 'He'll be terrified. Having you there could help.'

The room was on the second floor. There was a sagging bed, a battered dresser, a chair, a night table, and a sink with a mirror above it. There was a small lamp on the night table and another on the wall over the mirror. Even together, they cast only a dim light that left most of the room in shadow. The toilet was down the hall.

After a few minutes, there was a soft rap on the door. Willi opened the door.

Bobi looked up at Willi with wide, innocent eyes. He pursed his pouty lips, flirting as he'd been taught.

'This is Lola,' said Willi.

'OK,' said Bobi. 'I've done couples before. You want me to get undressed?'

'No,' said Willi. 'Just sit down for a minute.' He motioned toward the chair.

Bobi looked from Willi to Lola and back to Willi. 'Jesus. You're cops, aren't you?' He lunged for the door, but Willi was faster.

'Don't touch me, you filthy cop.'

Willi locked the door and stuck the key in his pocket. He went back to the bed and sat down. 'Sit down,' he said, pointing at the chair. *Just like a cop*, Lola thought.

'You can't keep me here, you know. In a half-hour, Bernie'll be back to get me, and he's going to kick your ass.'

'All you have to do is answer a few questions and you can go.'

'I'm not saying nothing.'

'You already told me about Bernie,' said Willi.

'Why is *she* here?' said Bobi.

Before Willi could speak, Lola said, 'Willi asked me to come. He thought you'd be scared of him, and I could help make you feel a little less—'

'I'm not scared of your little "Willi,"' said Bobi, with a sneer meant to prove the point.

'I can see you're not scared.' She turned to Willi. 'I told you it was ridiculous.'

Willi just shrugged.

'Bernie's going to kick your ass good,' said Bobi.

'I doubt he's all that tough,' said Willi.

Bobi looked Willi up and down, then snorted. 'Oh, he'll kick your ass all right.'

'Really?' said Willi, 'What makes you so sure?'

'How many guys have *you* killed, Willi? Huh?'

'A dozen,' said Willi.

Bobi looked at Willi. 'You're lying, right?'

'Yes,' said Willi and smiled. 'It's a joke.'

'You cops are all alike,' said Bobi.

'Willi wants to help you,' said Lola.

'They always say that, lady. Don't you know that? Right after they arrest you, they say that.'

'You have a lot of experience with the police?' said Willi.

'So what?' said Bobi.

'I suppose now you're going to tell me you've seen some bad cops.'

'Yeah. I have.'

How old are you, Bobi?'

'Eighteen,' said the boy. He looked young for twelve.

'Now you're just making stuff up,' said Willi. 'Name a bad cop, and if he's bad, I'll put him in jail.'

Bobi laughed. 'Not a chance.'

'Helmut Meier?' said Willi.

'Not him,' said Bobi. 'He's not bad. Just kind of pathetic.'

Willi named a few other cops. Bobi said he didn't know any of them.

When Lola asked Bobi about his parents, he called his mother a dirty bitch. He said she had abandoned him and his sister and brother. It turned out that she was an addict and had died of an overdose. He said his sister and brother, Anna and Franzl, were living with a mean uncle in Konstanz. Bobi was hustling for money to get Anna and Franzl out of there. 'I'm the oldest,' he said.

'How old?' said Lola.

This time he said, 'Thirteen. I'll be thirteen next month.'

'Who's the uncle in Konstanz?' said Willi.

'I'm not telling,' said Bobi.

'Uncle Ernst?' said Willi.

Bobi just looked at him like he was nuts.

Willi handed Bobi a ten-mark bill.

'What's this for?' said Bobi.

'For food. For Anna and Franzl. For whatever you need.'

Bobi looked at the bill and stuffed it in his back pocket. As soon as Willi unlocked the door, he was gone.

'Was that helpful?' Lola said.

'It was,' said Willi.

'How? He didn't tell you much.'

'He told me more than he thinks. And he'll stay in touch.'

'What makes you think so?' said Lola.

'He wants the money,' said Willi.

'What was that about Uncle Ernst?' said Lola.

'Just a shot in the dark. Something else I'm working on.'

An Excellent Witness

When Willi left the office the next evening, Bobi was waiting for him. 'What's up, Willi?' he said, as though they were old friends. He was after money, but there was something else about Willi: he didn't scare him.

When Willi brought up one of the cops he had named the night before, Bobi said, 'He likes to beat up kids.'

'Did he beat you up?' said Willi.

'Yeah,' said Bobi, trying to sound nonchalant. 'And he was laughing, and some other cops were laughing.' The boy blinked back tears. 'I'm going to kill them,' he said.

'No, you're not, Bobi,' said Willi. He put his hand on Bobi's shoulder.

Bobi shook it off angrily. 'Why shouldn't I?' he said. 'They're a bunch of Nazis.'

'Were they all cops?'

'Yeah.'

'And they're Nazis?'

'Don't you believe me?'

'I believe you, Bobi. There are lots of Nazis that are cops. And there are lots of bad men that are cops. But not all the bad men were Nazis. Some are just bad men. Like Bernie Pautsch.'

Bobi looked at Willi while he thought this over. 'Bernie wasn't a Nazi?'

'I don't think so,' said Willi.

'He acts like one,' said Bobi.

'What do you mean?' said Willi.

'Nothing,' said Bobi, and Willi let it go.

Bobi now lived with some other children in a bombed-out school building. He had moved there so Bernie couldn't find him. He didn't want to go with men anymore.

Bobi showed up regularly, catching Willi coming from work or leaving home. And he talked freely about working for Bernie and what he knew about the business. There were several black marketeers involved, including an American army sergeant and a chief of detectives in Nürnberg, but no one that sounded like Werner Krosius.

'What do you do with the money I give you, Bobi?' Willi asked one day.

'I told you. I put it away.'

'Where?' said Willi.

'Where it's safe,' said Bobi. 'You think I'm stealing your money, don't you? Go to hell, Willi. You're like all the rest.'

Bobi stopped showing up. After a week, Willi went looking for him and found him lying on a rotten mattress in the bombed-out school. His face was battered and bruised, his left eye was swollen shut, and his nose looked broken. 'Who did this, Bobi?'

Bobi turned to face the wall.

'Open your shirt,' said Willi.

'Leave me alone,' said Bobi.

'Open your shirt, or I'll do it for you,' said Willi.

Bobi did as he was told. His entire body was covered with black and blue bruises. 'Did he take your money, Bobi?'

'I don't know what you mean,' said Bobi. He didn't know how to stop being a tough guy.

'Did Bernie take the money for Anna and Franzl?'

Bobi looked at Willi with rage on his battered face. Then slowly his face dissolved. His jaw trembled. His eyes filled with tears that then coursed down his cheeks, making tracks through the dust and grime. When Willi took hold of his thin arms, Bobi threw his arms around Willi's neck and sobbed.

The Law

The only evidence Willi had that Bernie Pautsch was a killer was the word of a pervert and a twelve-year-old street kid. The night clerk was more frightened of Bernie than he was of Willi, so he had stopped talking. After all, he had only handed customers a room key. There was nothing illegal about that. He didn't know they were perverts, and Willi couldn't prove otherwise. Plus, the customers all used fake names, and now they had all disappeared.

The number you called when you wanted to reserve a boy was a public phone in the train station. Willi had heard the trains being announced. A waiter in the nearby café was paid to answer the phone. Then he called another number with the customer's information, and someone called the customer back.

Willi hauled the waiter in. The waiter said he did it for the money that showed up in an envelope every two weeks. When Willi showed him mug shots of Bernie and Helmut and a few others, he couldn't identify anyone. Yes, he figured the people on the phone were making sex dates, but he didn't know it was children. 'I swear,' he said. 'My wife and I have a twelve-year-old and an eight-year-old.' He was telling the truth about the wife and kids. And Willi believed the guy.

There was just no hard evidence to lock Bernie up on, and nothing that a smart lawyer couldn't get thrown out of court. But after Bernie beat up Bobi, Willi decided to arrest him anyway.

Bernie lived in a spacious apartment in a fancy building on a fancy block. The bombs hadn't spared the neighborhood, and Willi had to pick his way between piles of rubble to get to the building. Willi showed his badge to the concierge who picked up the phone. 'Don't call him,' said Willi. 'And if I find out you did, I'll arrest you. Now, is he here?'

'I don't know.'

'I'll ask you once more: is he here?' said Willi, getting right up in the man's face.

'He came in a little while ago,' he said.

Willi rang the bell. It was a while before Bernie came to the door.

'What do you want?' he said.

'You're under arrest,' said Willi and pushed his way inside.

Bernie grabbed a revolver from the table beside the door, but Willi already had his own pistol out and smacked Bernie on the side of the head with it. Bernie wobbled but didn't let go of the revolver, so Willi smacked him again. Willi grabbed the revolver as Bernie went down, out cold. Willi got cuffs on him behind his back and tied his shoelaces together before he came to.

He found the phone and called for a police ambulance. Bernie stayed in the hospital under guard for three days, which was enough time for Willi to have ballistics fire Bernie's pistol into a barrel of water and discover that it was the weapon that had killed the pawnbroker.

These days you didn't know what would and wouldn't stand up in court. The legal system left over from the Third Reich was supposedly becoming a 'new' legal system, while many of the judges, lawyers, administrators, and police remained in place. Nazi lawyers, judges, and administrators became newborn democrats.

Bernie Pautsch was represented in court by Lukas Pettermann who embodied this smooth, necessary, and bizarre transformation. Pettermann had earned his law degree in Cologne in 1940 and ran a small practice during the Third Reich, doing mostly real estate and financial transactions. But his career took off after the war ended, thanks to his work on behalf of two defendants in the Nürnberg trials. One was a former judge who, Pettermann argued, had been obliged to judge cases under existing law, and therefore had been doing his legal duty when he participated in the rounding up and execution of members of Operation Walküre. The other was the commandant of a concentration camp for whom Pettermann made a similar argument that he was just doing his duty. To have done otherwise would have been a violation of his oath of allegiance to the existing and legitimate government of Germany. To say now that the Third Reich was a criminal enterprise was changing the law after the fact. Both men were convicted and sentenced to prison terms by the Allied judges, but they were not executed as they could have been, and Pettermann's defense was credited with that.

Lukas Pettermann didn't come cheap these days and didn't usually take on out-and-out thugs like Bernie Pautsch. But there he was at Bernie's arraignment. Pettermann tried to assert that the gun had been illegally obtained by the police, so that any evidence having to do with the gun could not be used in court. He said also that the arrest had been improperly conducted, that the arresting policeman – Detective Willi Geismeier – had failed to identify himself, and that his client Mr Pautsch had taken him to be an intruder. When all that failed, he argued that his client, a substantial member of the community, should not be held in prison, but should be released on his own recognizance. That failed, too, and Bernie was held in jail to be tried on the charge of murder, among other crimes.

Captain Breuer congratulated Willi on bringing the case to a successful close. Willi assured him it was far from closed, since he believed that running an enterprise such as the child prostitution ring was far above Bernie Pautsch's capabilities. Bernie was a strong arm, but someone bigger than Bernie was pulling the strings, and in fact the trafficking of children continued under different management. He also thought that some of the lawyer's arguments, particularly the improper nature of the arrest, might lead to an acquittal. 'And,' he added, 'Pettermann's got more tricks up his sleeve.'

'Well,' said Breuer, 'it's out of our hands now.' Willi didn't think so, but he kept that opinion to himself. He also didn't say he thought there might be a trail leading to Werner Krosius. He had no evidence for that other than Krosius's past habit of having a finger in criminal enterprises all over Bavaria. Where there was money to be made, Krosius was not far off.

Willi sat waiting at a table in a small windowless holding cell off the reception area that was used for meetings at the Landberg Prison where Bernie was being held. Willi had asked to meet with Bernie Pautsch, and Lukas Pettermann had agreed to allow a meeting, as long as there were no questions about or relating to the murder of the pawnbroker. And that included questions about the child-trafficking ring.

Pettermann kept Willi waiting for an hour. Willi was used to such tactics and always had a book with him. This time it was Shakespeare's sonnets. He laid it aside as the two men came into the cell.

Pettermann shook hands with Willi while Bernie glowered. The lawyer reiterated which questions he would not allow. Willi said again that was fine with him. Then he began. 'Herr Pautsch, do you know someone named Werner Krosius?'

A look of surprise crossed the lawyer's face. 'Why are you asking him that?' he said.

Now it was Willi's turn to be surprised. 'I'm asking for my own reasons,' said Willi. 'Why? Shouldn't I? Does Werner Krosius have something to do with the murder of the pawnbroker or the trafficking of children?'

Pettermann realized he had made a mistake and said, 'No, there's no reason you shouldn't ask.' He turned toward Bernie and said, 'You can answer the question.' But Willi could see that was a little play-acting meant to cover Pettermann's unease.

'Never heard of him,' said Bernie.

'Werner Krosius was heavily involved in the black market during the war,' said Willi. 'He was in Passau for a time. You know Passau, don't you, Herr Pautsch?'

'I was born there,' said Bernie. 'But I got out of that hole when I was sixteen.'

'And you came here to Munich when you left Passau, didn't you?' said Willi.

'So?' said Bernie.

'Why did you come here?' said Willi.

'It was the big city,' said Bernie. 'I came here to find work.'

'You got work as a policeman, didn't you?'

'Yeah.'

'And you were thrown off the force, weren't you? Why was that?'

'I don't remember,' said Bernie.

'You were running a small black-market operation, weren't you?'

Bernie shrugged.

'And you were extorting people you arrested, weren't you?'

'You looked it all up, so why are you asking?' said Bernie.

'It brings me back to Werner Krosius,' said Willi. 'He was running a big black-market operation at the same time, selling all sorts of big-ticket stuff – drugs, commodities – in Passau, in Munich, among other places. He also sold plundered Jewish art. He's supposed to have sold some paintings to Hermann Goering.'

Bernie looked up sharply. That rang a bell. 'Come to think of it,' he said, 'I *do* remember hearing something about a guy selling pictures . . .'

Pettermann interrupted Bernie. 'Don't answer that, Herr Pautsch. The detective is on a fishing expedition, and if you're not careful, you'll end up caught in the net yourself.'

Bernie looked at the lawyer sharply. 'What do you mean?' He thought he might have information he could trade for leniency or even some charges being dropped.

'I'm sorry, Herr Pautsch, but I have to end this interview right now. For your own protection.'

'What . . .?' said Bernie. 'Wait. What are you offering, Detective?'

'Guard!' said Pettermann, standing up and stepping in front of Bernie. 'Guard! We're finished here!' The guard who was standing nearby came up, took Bernie by the arm, and walked him back to his cell. Then Pettermann gave Willi a scathing look, turned on his heel, and walked out.

Willi sat alone for a minute considering what had just happened. After turning different scenarios over in his mind, he came to the conclusion that maybe the road to Werner Krosius led not through Bernie Pautsch, but through Lukas Pettermann.

Lukas Pettermann

Willi searched police records, court filings, and civil records to learn what he could about Lukas Pettermann's legal cases. He didn't expect to find Krosius mentioned by name. But he hoped to find records that somehow pointed to Krosius. He struck gold when he found Pettermann's flamboyant signature at the bottom of some records of several substantial currency and property transfers between 'unnamed entities.' Some were transfers of money to Swiss banks, so there was nothing more to be learned there. But some of the properties in question were in Munich, Passau, and Nürnberg, and these were instructive.

The Passau transfer of an apartment on Prinzregentenstraße caught Willi's eye. A quick check revealed it was Krosius's old apartment. The exchange had happened around the time Willi and Krosius had met. Tax documents revealed that the apartment had been transferred twice on the same day, first by its undisclosed owner to a limited liability corporation, Stift GmbH, and then to another undisclosed purchaser. It was a cash transaction.

Another interesting transaction was the sale of the Hotel Zentral in Munich. It too had its ownership transferred from an undisclosed entity to Stift GmbH, which then sold it for cash to an undisclosed new owner the same day. Stift GmbH had bought and sold multiple properties, always after a transfer by unnamed entities and always for cash. And when Willi searched for registry and tax documents on Stift GmbH, the company did not seem to exist.

Willi consolidated what he had found into a thick folder to show Hans Bergemann. Bergemann knew more about embezzlement, money laundering, and financial crimes than Willi did. It was a Thursday evening, and the restaurant where they met was nearly empty. The waiter had taken their order and now stood near the kitchen fussing with silverware. Willi sipped his beer while Bergemann leafed back and forth through the pages. 'I'm not sure you've got anything on Krosius here,' said Bergemann. 'What were you hoping for?'

'Well,' said Willi, 'I've got this murder that looks like an execution, and the murderer comes up with a fancy lawyer. And the fancy lawyer has done a number of big deals, at least one of which – the apartment – ties him directly to Werner Krosius, a black marketeer who may also be tied to the murder of an American pilot and Fedor Blaskowitz. Except the black marketeer is supposedly dead and . . .'

'And,' Bergemann interrupted, '*and* the killing of the pilot and Fedor were an act of war, so even if this Krosius is alive *and* involved, which you're guessing at, it's not a punishable crime.'

'But the trafficking of children is; the execution of the pawnbroker is.'

'But you're just guessing that Krosius is involved,' said Bergemann.

'*Meine Herren!*' said the waiter, presenting their suppers, as waiters often do, just at the moment when the conversation needed to continue. Willi and Bergemann leaned back to make room for the plates, and Bergemann closed the folder and put it aside. '*Das Schnitzel?*' said the waiter.

'Here,' said Bergemann.

'*Kalbsleber?*'

'*Danke*,' said Willi. He and Bergemann wished each other '*Guten Appetit!*' and then ate in silence.

Finally, Bergemann picked up the thread again. 'You think Krosius is responsible for Fedor's death, but you have no evidence that he is. And you have just as little evidence that he's involved in the murder of the pawnbroker. And you want to frame him for the one to punish him for the other. Have I got that right?'

Willi laughed. 'Not quite,' he said. 'Let's talk about the law for a minute, can we?'

Bergemann rolled his eyes.

Willi ignored the gesture and began by reminding Bergemann that the new German criminal justice system was largely made up of the same people that had made up the old one. And the laws, particularly the criminal code, remained more or less the same as they had been during the Third Reich. Murder then was murder now; embezzlement then was embezzlement now. 'Now, the interesting thing – the thing that's important in light of the current case . . .' Willi paused and waited for Bergemann to say there was no case.

Instead, Bergemann said how delicious and tender his *Schnitzel* was and pretended not to be listening.

Willi smiled but was not distracted. 'The interesting thing we forget sometimes is that the *criminal* system hasn't changed either. The people who were criminals in 1941 are still criminals after the Third Reich is past, now – December 1945 – and will continue to be criminals in 1946 and beyond. And their network is still there. Bernie Pautsch was a thug and a pimp then, and he still is. The pawnbroker was a fence and a cheat then, and he still was when Bernie killed him. It's as if the shift from the Third Reich to the new Germany hasn't even happened for them. Bernie and the pawnbroker and everyone like them are part of a system, too – a crime system, you could say, with lots of interconnecting elements. It may not be codified the way the legal system is, but it's a system all the same, with its own rules, its own customs and traditions, and it continues. Krosius was a black marketeer and a general criminal opportunist before the war and through the war. He was engaged in financial crimes then. I believe he was involved in prostitution and human trafficking then. What reason is there to think he's a law-abiding citizen now? How could that even happen? The black market still thrives; the money is still laundered.'

'If he's even alive,' said Bergemann.

'If he's alive, he'll be connected to his past somehow, despite his efforts to cut the connection. Anyway, his crimes are still alive. None of that just goes away. And it should be prosecuted.'

'If you can find him,' said Bergemann.

'Well, we've found Pettermann,' said Willi.

'Krosius will be harder,' said Bergemann. 'If he's alive, he'll have changed his identity. He might be in Australia or Timbuktu, for all you know.'

'I've had several different identities, as you know, Hans. And the one thing I learned is that changing your identity is only possible if no one is looking for you.'

'The point of this lecture?'

'The point is Krosius is a criminal. He laundered large sums of money. I believe he faked his own death. None of which suggests he has suddenly gone straight. And none of it suggests he meant to leave Germany. He's still a criminal, and I suspect he's still in Germany. Getting him for whatever crimes he's committed will be as good as getting him for Fedor and for Charlie Herder's death.'

'As good?'

'Yes. As good. In case you're asking, yes, it's personal.'

Director General Georg Berghof

The secretary knocked on Georg Berghof's office door.

'Come in,' he said. He laid aside the papers he had been reading. 'What is it?' he said.

'I'm sorry to bother you, Herr Director General. But Herr Pettermann is calling.'

'Thank you, Gerda,' said Georg. He picked up the phone. 'What is it?' he said.

'We should meet,' said Pettermann.

Krosius had been Director General Georg Berghof since Werner Krosius had 'died' in the bombing of Passau. Allied Development GmbH had come into existence not long after. Its offices were in a building across the street from the Max Planck Institute in Berlin, a building Krosius had bought with laundered money. Allied Development consisted in its entirety of a brass plate on the front of the building, a suite of offices with a conference room, the Director General, and his secretary, Gerda Drechsler. There were no other employees, there were no products, and no company business was conducted.

Gerda had previously been the madam in a whorehouse in Augsburg that Krosius had been involved in. The whorehouse had been exceptionally profitable under Gerda's capable leadership. She was loyal and trustworthy, and when the time came to kill off Krosius and start anew, he had brought her along. At first, there was little for her to do. She answered the occasional phone call, filed a few papers, typed letters now and then. The job was boring – the Herr Director did most of the paperwork himself – but he paid her well, mostly for her complicity and discretion. You couldn't have a Director General without a secretary.

Krosius had been interested in SS Lieutenant Laumann because knowing Laumann and accommodating him had made it possible for Krosius to move goods and to meet with other criminals in the open and unimpeded. His couriers and operatives had passes

from the SS. But eventually, Laumann had pressed him for more
and more information. He was particularly interested in the
Flower Gang.

When Laumann discovered that some of the Flower Gang
information was invented, he decided that Krosius should bring
more than just names and places to the game. Krosius should be
involved in the operation itself: the roundup of the American
pilot and as many of the Flower Gang as possible. Krosius should
have skin in the game.

'Out of the question, Lieutenant,' said Krosius. 'I've given
you abundant information you couldn't get on your own – names,
places. And what have you done with it? Nothing. These flower
people are still operating at will.'

'You see, Krosius, that's where you're wrong. Despite the false
information you've fed me, I've built a case and set a trap. And
now you're going to help me spring that trap.'

'I don't see why,' said Krosius. 'I don't see any benefit to me.'

'The benefit to you, Herr Krosius, is that you are able to
avoid being arrested and sent to Dachau. You may even continue
trading contraband, moving money, trafficking in sex, and all
the rest of your unsavory activities.'

Krosius had learned too late, like so many businessmen, legitimate and illegitimate, that cooperation with the Third Reich
always took you deeper into their world than you had ever meant
to go. He resisted Laumann's threats a while longer, but then
agreed that he would assemble the people to carry out the
operation.

'They have to be reliable,' said Laumann.

'Reliable?'

'Politically reliable. Loyal to the Führer and capable of doing
what needs to be done.'

'Gangsters, in other words.'

Laumann just shrugged.

Krosius had known Ernst Nutzke both by reputation and from
the trading business. Laumann had explained exactly what he
wanted Nutzke to do – intercept the Flower Gang and the pilot
on their way to the border, arrest them, and then the Gestapo
would do the rest. Krosius told Ernst there were a thousand
Reichsmarks in it. Nutzke jumped at the chance. Krosius could

see that Nutzke wasn't interested in just arresting them. He meant to rough them up. But that was Laumann's problem.

When the arrest turned into a massacre, Laumann blamed Krosius and saw to it that word filtered up to the German High Command that Krosius was poison. Krosius's deals selling weapons from the Russian battlefield had already become extremely problematic. It had poisoned his name in some circles. After the massacre, not even the *Reichsmarschall* would take his calls. Laumann was pleased. He had killed two birds – the Flower Gang and Krosius – with one stone. Of course, any hope that Laumann would ever be promoted to major was over, too.

Krosius had taken the only way out. He had known the day would come, and he was prepared. He had liquidated what he could, had cleaned up the money, and had constructed a new identity as Director General Georg Berghof, a Berlin businessman. He had considered leaving Germany, but then American money had started pouring in – money for reconstruction, money to build up the new capitalist democracy, money to fight the Soviet Union and the communist menace – and that money was irresistible to Werner Krosius.

Pettermann, having just arrived on the overnight train, met the Director General in a seedy cabaret near the Bahnhof Zoo, the Berlin train station. They had never met in person, and the Director General had preferred to keep it that way. 'What's the reason for this meeting?' he said as they sat down at a corner table.

'The phones are unsafe,' said Pettermann.

'And what's so important?' said the Director General.

'Detective Willi Geismeier,' said Pettermann.

The Director General remembered Willi. 'Herr Schacht,' he said.

'Who?' said Pettermann.

'It's a Geismeier alias. It's a long story,' said the Director General.

'Anyway, Geismeier, a police detective now, interviewed Pautsch in the Landberg Prison. He asked Pautsch about you.'

'Pautsch doesn't know me, right? He doesn't know who's paying for his defense?'

'No.'

'So what's the problem?'

'Pautsch is eager to make a deal to stay out of prison. And Geismeier is asking about you and the child-trafficking thing.'

'But you said we're out of that, Pettermann. So what are you telling me? Are we out of that or not?'

'Yes, you're out of it. *Now* you're out of it. But you *were* in it not too long ago, Herr Director. And your past doesn't just go away.'

The Lutz Connection

The roof was gone, but the Dornier factory still stood, and the tall window frames were still in place on the ruined walls. The giant machines remained, too, coated in dust and debris, like great, dead beasts. Drehfelderstraße was free of rubble now, but there were flat spaces where three apartment buildings had once stood. Their cellars had now been filled in. Number 120 still had the big crack in its facade, but someone had planted shrubs and a tree out front. The leaves were gone, so Willi couldn't tell what kind of tree it was.

Before going to Ballitz's apartment, Willi stopped to talk to Adolf Jobst. Adolf had enough to eat these days and had put on weight. He was at the university, taking courses in philosophy and literature. 'Frieda is in training to be a nurse,' he said. 'We never see the new people.' He nodded in the direction of Willi and Lola's old apartment. 'How is Frau . . . Zeff?' He had almost called her Frau Meier.

'She's fine,' said Willi. 'She works at the Mahogany Bar. Stop by and say hello. She'd love that, Adolf.'

'Elke came by,' said Adolf. 'She's interested in old Ballitz.'

Willi was surprised. 'Did she talk to him?'

'No, but she talked to Dietrich, the son.'

'What did she say about that?' said Willi.

'Nothing. I asked, but she wouldn't say anything. You know that little smile of hers. That's all I got.'

When Willi knocked on Ballitz's door, Frau Ballitz opened it a crack with the security chain still in place. 'Hello, Frau Ballitz. I'd like a word with Herr Ballitz, please.'

She closed the door, and a minute later she opened it again with the chain still in place.

'He doesn't want to talk to you,' she said.

'Tell him I'm the police,' said Willi. He showed her his badge.

She closed the door. When it opened again, Joachim Ballitz was there. He studied Willi's identification and badge, and finally took off the security chain. The apartment was large, but sparsely furnished. Willi could see where pictures were missing from the walls and carpets were gone from the floor. Ballitz had been out of work since Dornier had been destroyed, and the Ballitzes had been selling off their belongings little by little. His engineering skills were intact, but the last months of the war and the death of the Führer had broken him. He was thin and walked with a stoop. His hair was wispy and neglected. He hadn't shaved.

Willi asked when Ballitz had last had contact with Krosius. Earlier, Ballitz would have denied even knowing Krosius, would have been indignant at the implication that he knew such a person. But now he just said, 'I don't know. Not for a long time.'

'Since the end of the war?' said Willi.

'Oh, no, long before that. He gave me some *foie gras*.' The memory made his eyes light up, but the light went out just as quickly. 'That was long ago. And how are you, Herr Meier? And Frau Meier?'

'Fine, Herr Ballitz. We're both fine. And how's your son Dietrich, Herr Ballitz? Is he doing well?'

'My son? Dietrich? Oh, yes. He's doing very well.' Ballitz's mind was somewhere else.

Willi thanked Ballitz and said goodbye.

'Dietrich quit school,' said Frau Ballitz as she walked Willi to the door. 'He has a job with a freight company now. He says he wants to be an artist.' She shook her head as though it was all a mystery.

Willi found Dietrich at the freight company unloading a truck. He said he had ended all contact with his father. The gang of youngsters had broken up once the war ended. He was working this job so he could study art. He carried a pad of paper and pencils everywhere he went, and drew whenever he had a few minutes. Buildings, people, landscapes, whatever was in front of him.

Yes, Elke had found him and had asked him lots of questions. He had always admired her, he said, probably because his father hated her. But now he said he admired her for who she was, how she had endured.

She had asked him about any connections his father might have had in Konstanz. He didn't think he had any, but he couldn't be sure. She asked whether he knew where his father got the wine and cognac and *foie gras*. Several different people had delivered that stuff over the years. He remembered one guy who came fairly often – a beer-truck driver. He didn't remember his name. Egon, maybe? That sounded familiar to Willi. Only later would he come up with Egon Scharfheber.

Dietrich remembered there was one man who ran the business. He didn't remember his name, but he remembered his face. Dietrich took out paper and pencil and drew a quick likeness of Krosius – the wide-apart eyes, the innocent mouth, the neatly combed hair. It was him.

'Did you draw a picture of this man for Elke?' said Willi. Dietrich said he had.

'Did she recognize him?' said Willi.

'No, she didn't seem to.'

Then Dietrich drew a picture of the beer-truck driver. 'Erdinger Beer,' he said, remembering the truck.

When the war ended, Pierre had disappeared. Which meant Willi had to drive himself. He had an unmarked police car at his disposal. Bergemann agreed to go along, but only if he drove, which was fine with Willi. They found the Erdinger Beer depot with ease. 'Yes, Herr Scharfheber still works here,' said Hildegard. 'But he's out on deliveries.' She directed them to Herr Lutz the dispatcher. Lutz looked at the board and saw that Scharfheber was on his way to Passau.

'Is Passau on his regular route?' said Willi.

'The routes change from day to day,' said Lutz. 'But Egon goes there often enough. He likes going to Passau. I think there's a woman.'

'A woman?' said Bergemann.

'It's his weakness,' said Lutz. 'It's gotten him in trouble before.'

'How do you mean?' said Bergemann.

'With the SS. They used it against him to make him into a snitch. An SS lieutenant named Naumann or Laumann, something like that. Egon couldn't keep his mouth shut, always bragging about being in the SS. But I don't think he ever was.'

'Did you ever know a man named Werner Krosius?' said Willi.

Lutz stared at Willi for a long time before he said, 'No, I don't think so.'

Peter Steiner

'Herr Lutz, do you know the penalty for lying to a police officer in the course of a criminal investigation?'

Lutz stared at his hands for a very long time before looking up at Willi again. 'Look, Herr Detective: whatever he did in his life, Werner's dead now. He was Karin's only living relative. I'm only trying to protect her from any more pain.'

'Are you saying Krosius is your brother-in-law?' said Willi.

'Was,' said Lutz.

Herr Lutz had had very little to do with Krosius. He and Karin had accepted the small gifts that came their way from his black-market operation, but as the operation grew into something larger and more sinister – drugs and prostitution became part of it – they stopped having anything to do with him. 'The last thing I ever did for him was get him a ride to Passau on Scharfheber's truck. He was starting a new job in Passau. He convinced Karin he was turning over a new leaf. I only learned later that it was all a lie. The Passau job was a front. And Scharfheber was messing around in the black market himself.'

'And yet Scharfheber still works for you,' said Bergemann.

'Not for me. I don't hire or fire. That's Herr Annauer.'

'So, does Herr Annauer know about Scharfheber's past activities?'

'I have to assume he does,' said Lutz.

'Did he know Krosius was on the truck to Passau?'

'He was strict about allowing passengers on his trucks. But he gave permission for Krosius.'

'Did he know about Krosius's illegal activities?' said Bergemann.

'I don't really know what he knew,' said Lutz. 'But I assume he did.'

'Changing the subject, Herr Lutz,' said Willi, 'did you know anything about underground operations around here?'

Lutz gave Willi that long stare again.

'I'll take that as a "yes," Herr Lutz.'

Lutz sighed. 'I heard there was an American pilot holed up nearby for a while. He and some others were ambushed when they tried for the Swiss border. One of them was supposedly a schoolteacher over in Murnau. Karin and I talked about it not too long ago. She thought she met the schoolteacher once. We couldn't come up with his name.'

'Fedor Blaskowitz?' said Willi.

'Right. That was it. Is that what you're investigating, Herr Detective? The ambush, I mean?'

'That's part of it, Herr Lutz. It's complicated.'

The Phone Call

F inding former SS Lieutenant Klaus Peter Laumann turned out to be pretty easy. He was living on his family's farm near Schwerin, close to the Baltic Sea, on that broad, open, uncomplicated landscape he had pined for the whole time he was in Bavaria. The trouble was, it was in the Soviet Zone, and the border was tightening by the day. So any contact between Willi and Laumann would have to be by letter or telephone.

To his surprise, Willi's letter to Klaus Peter Laumann got an immediate reply. Laumann wrote that he did not believe that the West German police were capable of dealing honestly with the crimes of the recent murderous fascist regime. He doubted that the corrupt capitalist, neo-fascist regime now in place could come to an honest reckoning. He wrote he was a devoted member of the Communist Party. However, he was willing to have a conversation with Detective Geismeier about the crimes he had witnessed during his forced service in the imperialist fascist German army during the recent war. The letter was signed Klaus Peter Laumann, Chairman, Klein Dieten Town Council, German Democratic Republic. The letter had been written with the Russian secret police in mind. Laumann meant to demonstrate that he had disavowed his errant ways and was a devoted communist official and loyal to the Soviet Union and the communist revolution.

In order to speak with Willi, Laumann would have to go to his local post office at the agreed-upon time and sign up to make a call to the West. He would have to wait for a line to be free, which could take an hour or longer. All calls were limited to five minutes. The lines between East and West Germany were in high demand as families and businesses torn apart by the division into zones of occupation tried to make arrangements or do business or simply stay in touch.

It went without saying that Laumann's call to Willi would be monitored by the Russian secret police, the NKGB. That was the reason Laumann agreed to make the call. It was a chance to demonstrate again his loyalty to the communist revolution. Of course, the American National Intelligence Authority would be listening, too, along with the Reinhard Gehlen Organization, the fledgling West German intelligence agency. But that only made Laumann's loyalty all the more compelling.

Not long after the agreed-upon time, Willi's phone rang. It was Laumann. He began with a speech. Yes, Werner Krosius should be held responsible for his various crimes. He had enriched himself by exploiting the hardworking masses. However, the neo-fascists that Willi served would find neither the means nor the resolve to bring a class enemy like Krosius to justice. Doing so would require them to recognize that Krosius was the product and the embodiment of the corrupt capitalist system. If Krosius was to be punished, then the whole system should be dismantled. They were one and the same.

Willi asked how Laumann had come to know Werner Krosius. Laumann said Krosius had tried to enlist his support in his various schemes – prostitution, black market – and he, Laumann, had always resisted.

Willi asked whether Laumann had been involved in any way in the murder of the American pilot Charles Herder or the resister Fedor Blaskowitz. Laumann answered that while it was true that he had been manipulated and duped into wearing the uniform of the corrupt and evil fascist regime, he had not committed any crimes against the working class and did not know anything about any American pilot or resister.

Willi said he had heard Krosius was killed in an air raid in Passau. 'Is that true?' he said.

'I can't say,' said Laumann.

'You can't say? Or you don't know?' said Willi.

Willi imagined all the other people listening and waiting for the correct answer.

After a pause, Laumann said, 'I don't know.'

That sounded to Willi like the correct answer.

Mr West

The morning after Willi's conversation with Laumann, the lawyer Pettermann called. He apologized for not calling sooner. Willi said he had originally called because Pettermann had given him the impression that he might know a man named Werner Krosius. Willi said he thought Krosius, who had been involved in various criminal enterprises during the Nazi era, might still be involved in such crimes, particularly the child-trafficking ring he was currently investigating. He had a few questions about Werner Krosius that he hoped the lawyer could help him clear up. 'Do you know Werner Krosius?'

Pettermann was not rattled. Instead, he said, 'I am more than happy to answer all your questions, Herr Geismeier. I will tell you everything I know. But not on the telephone.' Pettermann proposed that Willi should come to meet him the next morning. He gave him an address on Schillerstraße near the train station.

'Is Krosius dead?' said Willi.

'Until tomorrow at nine,' said Pettermann and hung up the phone.

The day was cold, and an east wind was blowing. It was sunny one minute, and clouds skidded in front of the sun the next. Willi had on a heavy scarf and his thick tweed coat for the first time this winter. The coat smelled of mothballs. He wore new prescription sunglasses, too. 'You have the start of cataracts,' his opthamologist had warned him. Time marches on, thought Willi.

Willi walked the three kilometers to Schillerstraße. He didn't think he would ever get enough of walking freely through the streets of Munich without being chased, shadowed, or otherwise in fear for his life. He arrived at the Schillerstraße address a little before nine and stopped for a coffee across the street in a little standup café.

Willi had assumed the meeting would be in Pettermann's office, but this building was under construction and looked unoccupied. The walls were raw block, and the windows had tape and labels across them. Willi crossed the street and pushed the button for 5B. A voice said, 'Yes?' He said his name and was buzzed in.

There were construction materials in the small lobby, a wheelbarrow filled with debris, and a concrete staircase. The place smelled like new concrete. Wires hung from the unfinished ceiling, waiting for lights. The lift was not working yet. By the time he had reached the fifth floor, he was a little out of breath. There was more construction debris in the hallway. Most of the offices had their doors wide open and were unoccupied. Number 5B had a steel door. Willi knocked, and the door opened with the security chain attached; a man looked out, then closed the door to remove the chain.

Pettermann was waiting inside. He was seated, still wearing his coat and holding a briefcase on his lap. He stood up, smiled, and offered Willi his hand. 'Detective Geismeier, thank you for coming,' he said. 'This is Mr West.'

'*Guten Tag*,' said the man who had opened the door. He offered Willi his hand. He gestured for Willi to sit down on one of the chairs at a small conference table. 'We're just moving in,' he said with a thick American accent, 'but the damned heat isn't working yet.' He grinned and blew a puff of steam to prove it. Mr West wore wool slacks, a white shirt, and no jacket, despite the cold. In fact, his sleeves were rolled up and his necktie was loosened, the way Americans liked to do, maybe, Willi thought, to show everyone how busy they were.

Pettermann kept his coat on and moved to the conference table. He opened the briefcase and took out a thick manilla file. Willi took the pad out of his coat pocket where he had written all his questions, although he now had a whole new set.

'You want some coffee?' said Mr West in English.

'No, thanks,' said Willi.

'I've got pretty good German, Detective,' said Mr West, 'but I hear you speak perfect English. I know Pettermann can manage in English, so it would be a big help if we could speak English.'

'That's fine with me,' said Willi.

'So, Detective, I hear you're interested in Werner Krosius, a dead man, in connection with a sex-crime ring.'

'Among other things,' said Willi.

'Well, we can get to the other things later. But the sex-crime thing: I understand you've got your man . . .' He searched for the name.

'Bernhard Pautsch,' said Pettermann.

'You've got Pautsch in prison, you've got an open-and-shut case against him for murder and trafficking. Krosius has been dead for over a year. There's no evidence he was ever involved in any of this in any way. So, I wonder why you're interested in him.'

'Well, to start with, I'm not convinced Krosius is dead,' said Willi.

Pettermann went into the file in front of him, took out a copy of a death certificate, and slid it across the table.

Willi glanced at the certificate but didn't study it. 'What else have you got?' he said.

'What do you mean?' said Mr West.

Willi took his Swedish passport for Walter Meier out of his pocket. He still carried it sometimes; it came in handy. He opened it to the page with his picture on it and slid it across the table to Mr West. 'My passport,' he said.

West picked it up, studied it, then smiled. 'All right, Detective,' he said. 'There are fake documents. You made your point.'

'Not quite,' said Willi. 'Here's my point: Pautsch, a fairly low-order murderer, shows up with a fancy lawyer – Pettermann here – and when it occurs to me to wonder whether Werner Krosius might be paying for Pettermann's services, Pettermann – sorry, Herr Pettermann – goes all pale and trembly. I have to wonder why, don't I?'

There was no response from Pettermann or Mr West, so Willi continued. 'Krosius is a major criminal. As he was during the war – black market, human trafficking, and more. Maybe accessory to murder. And now he could be somehow involved in a ring that prostitutes children. That seems to me to be worth pursuing. I have to believe that in the United States a child trafficker, a black marketeer, a war profiteer, an accessory to more than one murder would be vigorously pursued, arrested, and prosecuted.

'And now here I sit, in this pretend office with someone I can only take to be an American secret agent of some kind or other. So I have to wonder not only where Krosius is, but why he's being protected, and by whom.'

Throughout his little speech, Willi had watched the rage build in the man who called himself Mr West. He had been scowling and the muscles in his jaw were flexing. And now he exploded. 'By *whom*?! *BY WHOM*?! I'll tell you by fucking *WHOM*. The people *WHOM* kicked your fucking Nazi ass, Herr Detective. I don't know what *you* did these last five years, how many people you sent to fucking Dachau, how many Jews you fucking killed, where you goose-stepped around in your fucking uniform. And frankly I don't give a shit.

'Maybe Krosius is everything you say he is; maybe he's even worse. I don't give a shit about that either. In case you haven't noticed, these are fucking perilous times, Geismeier.' (*Perilous?* thought Willi. *Who says 'perilous' anyway?*) Mr West went on. 'For you, the war is over. Hooray. But a hundred miles east of here, the fucking communist Russian army is digging in, setting up artillery in permanent emplacements, and getting ready to start the next fucking war. We're in a standoff with the Soviet Union right now, and they're working on a fucking atom bomb, Geismeier. And we'd better do everything we can, and I mean *everything*, to keep them in check, or our ass is grass. Some of the stuff we do isn't gonna be pretty. Some of the people we use aren't gonna be nice people.

'So here's the long and short of it, Geismeier. The man you call Werner Krosius is dead as far as you're concerned. Because – believe me – you're never getting anywhere near him. Never. And if you know what's good for you, you'll stop looking for him. If I ever hear you're still trying, I'll have your ass. So help me, Geismeier, I'll have your ass. Go ahead and lock up Bernhard Pautsch and throw away the fucking key for all I care. But don't even think of going after Krosius, or we'll come down on you like a fucking hammer. I hope you understand me, Herr Detective. Now, if you don't have any more fucking questions, get the fuck out of here. I have a plane to catch.'

Willi leafed back and forth through his notebook as though he were looking for questions. 'No,' he said. 'No more questions.'

The Trial

I
t had taken nearly four months to get Bernie Pautsch's trial on the docket, but in March 1946 he was brought up before three judges. The charges were murder, human trafficking, embezzlement, and racketeering.

The presiding judge had been a devout Nazi in the twenties and through most of the thirties. But in 1939, he had finally had enough and had left the country for Brazil. He had only recently returned, encouraged by the Americans who were looking for relatively untainted judges to fill vacancies on the bench. The two other judges had stayed in Germany throughout but had managed to keep their heads down, or at least to keep their records clean.

Willi had stopped his active pursuit of Werner Krosius and now occupied himself with other cases as they crossed his desk. He still followed leads on the child-trafficking case as they presented themselves. Bobi had helped him turn up one observant and talkative witness, a cabaret actor who had ruined his career and whose entire family had turned on him because of his sins. Talso – he was one of those showmen who use just one name – felt genuine remorse and wanted nothing more than to make amends for the wrongs he had done. Thanks to his voluminous testimony and irrefutable evidence, the ring unraveled. Sixteen people were indicted, including the mastermind of the operation, a former police official, who was now in a cell not far from Bernie Pautsch. They met sometimes in the yard during their daily exercise and pretended not to know each other. Willi received a commendation for his work. Of course, the money behind the operation remained a mystery.

Once the trial began, Willi went as often as he could. He was particularly interested to see what kind of defense Pettermann would mount. Pettermann called alibi witnesses who said Bernie had been elsewhere, but whose testimony fell apart under the judges' questioning. He presented a witness

who said that the revolver that killed the pawnbroker was not
Bernie's. On cross-examination, the witness had to admit the
revolver had been in Bernie's possession when he was arrested.
And several prosecution witnesses testified that he had had it
with him the day of the pawnbroker's killing.

Rolf Fasan the purse snatcher testified that he had seen Bernie
leaving the pawnshop the day of the murder. Bernie glowered
at Rolf, but Rolf stuck to his story under Pettermann's insufficient
cross-examination. Pettermann's halfhearted and incompetent
defense puzzled Willi until he realized that Pettermann was
trying to lose the case.

Willi was called to give evidence. The judges had heard
Pettermann's various objections to Bernie's treatment by the
police, and now they wanted to hear Willi's version of it. Given
the moment in history and the judges' own personal histories,
they were, not surprisingly, sensitive to allegations of police
abuses of every kind.

Willi began by giving his name, rank, address, and other
information as witnesses were always required to do. Then the
presiding judge got right down to business. 'Detective Geismeier,'
he said, 'how long have you been a policeman?'

'I have been a policeman three different times, Herr Judge,'
said Willi. 'Very briefly before the Great War, then from 1917
until I was dismissed in 1930, and most recently since July 1945,
so about nine months this time. That adds up to about fifteen
years. So far.'

'I see,' said the judge. 'And, Detective, how did you spend
the years between 1930 and 1945?'

The judges had never seen or heard of Willi before, so it was
natural they could imagine Willi might try to whitewash his Nazi
years.

'Herr Judge,' said Willi, 'I was a criminal.' The judges stared
at him with raised eyebrows. 'By which I mean,' said Willi, 'I
was outside the law. I was pursued by the SS and the Gestapo
for subverting their efforts, for helping Jews and political enemies
of the state to escape from Germany, that sort of thing.'

All three judges stared at Willi. The presiding judge poured
himself a glass of water and drank it slowly. The other two
regretted that he had beaten them to it, because they both felt

their throats go dry as they considered their own histories. And three judges drinking water at the same time would have looked comical.

'Detective,' said the presiding judge finally, 'the defendant has claimed that you assaulted him when you arrested him, causing him grievous injury, and that your arrest was illegal since you did not have a warrant.'

'*Herr Richter*, it's true, I did cause the defendant serious injury. He had a revolver and was about to shoot me. Hitting him with my own pistol was the only way to stop him. When he fell, I was able to take his revolver and put him in restraints. I immediately called for an ambulance, and he was taken to the hospital.'

'And the lack of a warrant, Herr Detective?'

'We had been aware of the defendant and his crimes for some time, *Herr Richter*, but didn't have enough evidence to make an arrest. We had been searching for evidence as we were searching for his criminal partners. When we learned he had beaten up a child, a twelve-year-old boy, we decided we had to arrest him. He was a threat to the child and presented an imminent danger. There was not enough time to get a warrant.'

One of the other judges chimed in. 'And has your search for others in the child-trafficking ring borne fruit, Herr Detective? Have you found any other participants in Herr Pautsch's gang?'

'Herr Judge, I object.' Pettermann stood up. 'Your reference to the defendant's gang is prejudicial to my client. It jeopardizes his chances of getting a fair hearing in this court.'

The judges looked at Pettermann as though he were someone who had just wandered into the wrong courtroom. Pettermann saw their look and started to repeat his objection. But the presiding judge cut him off. 'Herr Pettermann,' he said, 'your objection is overruled. Herr Detective' – he turned to Willi – 'please answer the question.'

'Herr Pautsch did not lead us to any other members of his gang, Herr Judge. But you will have received reports of a number of arrests we have made recently in connection with the child-trafficking gang that includes the defendant. Mounting evidence proves that this gang is guilty of child abuse, trafficking, and other crimes.'

The first thing the judges discussed once they had withdrawn to consider their verdict was what one of them described as the 'lamentable' defense Pettermann had mounted. His reputation for imaginative defenses seemed undeserved, judging by his performance in this trial.

'On the other hand,' said the presiding judge, 'this was an open-and-shut case. A murder weapon, sound ballistic evidence, eyewitness testimony. What more could Pettermann have done?'

One of the other judges objected to the detective's unconventional methods. 'He's definitely skirting the law and ignoring normal legal procedures,' he said.

'Well,' said the other judge, 'that seems to be his way.' All three agreed that Detective Geismeier needed to be reined in.

Still, it took them less than thirty minutes to pronounce Bernard Pautsch guilty of murder, conspiracy, and human trafficking, and to sentence him to twenty years in prison.

'We'll appeal,' said Pettermann, putting his hand on Bernie's shoulder as they led him off. Bernie just glared at him. He didn't need to be a genius to know he had been set up.

The Man Who Couldn't Swim

Germany had been all but destroyed by the war. A million and a half bomber sorties had been flown over Germany; three million tons of bombs had been dropped. Whole cities had been bombed into ruin. Seventy-five percent of Hamburg was reduced to rubble. Sixty percent of Cologne, sixty percent of Dresden, seventy percent of Kassel, eighty percent of Mainz, eighty percent of Bochum. And around twenty million Germans – nearly one in three – were homeless.

People slept where they could. Concentration camps were turned into DP – displaced person – camps. The emptied barracks of Dachau now became home for thousands. Others lived in shanty towns or tents, or in caves carved out of the rubble itself.

That a boy of thirteen slept nights under tattered rags in the ruins of a convent – Bobi's most recent refuge – was not noteworthy. Willi or Lola saw to it that he was all right and had something to eat, so he was better off than many. When Willi had an extra mark or two, he gave it to Bobi. Bobi gave it right back to Willi to put with his savings, which were now in a bank account Willi had opened in Bobi's name.

'One of us should take him in,' said Lola one evening. Willi and Lola were still living apart. She had made a pot of soup with beans, potatoes, kale and other greens, flavored with bay leaves and a ham bone. They had eaten their fill, and Lola set the pot on the windowsill that served as her refrigerator. Willi said he had an early morning, but he wasn't quite ready to leave.

Willi had recently moved into a couple of rooms he had built in an abandoned warehouse that had once belonged to the company his grandfather had founded. You could still make out the faded blue sign – *GEISMEIER CERAMICS* – painted on the side of the building. Lola had helped him make the place livable.

'There are thousands like Bobi. We can't save them all,' said Willi.

'I'm not talking about saving anyone,' said Lola. 'I'm talking about a safe place to sleep. You have the room.'

'And his brother and sister, too, I suppose?' said Willi.

'Maybe,' said Lola. 'Why not?'

'And what about you?' said Willi. Lola wasn't sure she was ready to live together again. Plus, she would have a long streetcar ride to and from work. Willi said he had a police car at his disposal and could drive her. Then she said that she was willing to give living together a try. But she would take the streetcar.

The next weekend, Willi drove to Konstanz to meet Anna and Franzl, Bobi's sister and brother, and to talk with their foster parents. The Erdinger Brewery depot was not exactly on the way. But Willi knew that Egon Scharfheber had delivered contraband for Krosius. He had gone through his records and found the note from Daisy about Scharfheber being an SS informant.

Willi asked Bergemann to go with him. Bergemann drove.

Willi and Bergemann showed Scharfheber their police IDs, and Willi said they had a few questions.

Scharfheber got nervous right away. 'I was just a truck driver. I kept my head down. I didn't do anything . . .'

'Hey, relax, man,' said Bergemann. 'We heard you're a guy that knows his way around.'

'I don't really know,' said Scharfheber. He was having trouble adapting to the changing times.

Bergemann said their chief had sent them out to investigate some old story that, as far as they were concerned, was over and done with: the killing of a couple of people – an American pilot, a German traitor – people that, as far as he was concerned, probably needed killing. Bergemann said he had marched with the Führer. You had to if you knew what was good for you, wasn't that right? He said they had all just been serving their country, after all. The Führer had kept things on the straight and narrow, and now, when you got right down to it, it had all gone to shit. Bergemann was good at this sort of thing, and the fact that a lot of cops felt this way made it easy.

Scharfheber decided these cops were good guys, guys who understood the way things were. He said he wasn't really SS, but he had done what he could to help out. 'I knew about that killing. I had this pal; he came to me about it.'

'Who was this pal?' said Willi.

'A guy named Werner Krosius,' said Scharfheber.

'Man, you knew Werner?' said Bergemann, as though they were old friends. 'Man, old Werner was a real operator.'

'I'll say,' said Scharfheber. 'Werner and me, we did business all over Bavaria – Munich, Passau, Murnau, Konstanz. Legit business, I mean.'

'Sure. Of course,' said Bergemann.

'So, one day, Werner reaches out to me for help on an operation. They're going to shut down some underground types and he wants me to put together a team. I told him, no. I'm strictly in the intelligence field, I told him. Werner said he was helping out this SS lieutenant. Laumann. I knew this Laumann, did some work for him once myself. I said thanks, but no thanks. I was strictly intelligence.'

'But you found him somebody?' said Bergemann.

Scharfheber paused, eyed Bergemann, eyed Willi, and then thought, *What the hell; it's a good story.* 'So, I knew this guy over in Konstanz. Ernst Nutzke. Our paths had crossed more than once. It turned out Werner knew him, too. This kind of operation was right up Nutzke's alley.'

'Where's this guy Nutzke now?' said Willi.

Scharfheber held up his hand. He wasn't finished with his story. 'So Nutzke puts together this crew – a bunch of guys he knows, some from the border patrol, some friends. The SS arms them, and they lie in wait. Pretty soon, the pilot and the others show up. Nutzke and his crew surround them, and they're about to turn them over to the SS when the American grabs Nutzke's nephew and kills him with his own gun. Just like that. Blows his head off. Well, then it's all over; they shoot down the whole bunch of them: the American, a German guy – a schoolteacher – and a black girl. I don't know what the hell she was doing there, but good riddance. The SS arrives, takes Nutzke and the others back to headquarters, gives them each a thousand Reichsmarks, and sends them home.'

'Man!' said Bergemann. 'Who told you about it?'

'I got it from Nutzke himself,' said Scharfheber.

'No kidding? Is he still around?' said Willi.

'I haven't seen him for a while,' said Scharfheber. 'Last I knew, he was a customs agent in Konstanz.'

Ernst Nutzke's long criminal record had been expunged at the end of the war – probably thanks to Laumann. He hadn't been charged in Johann's or any other death. But he was drinking heavily. He had received an official warning that his position with German customs was in jeopardy, and he was on a police watch list.

Willi found Nutzke's sister, Johann's mother, in a two-room hovel behind the Marktstätte in Konstanz. She didn't want to know anything about Ernst Nutzke or talk about him either. He had murdered her son, she said, during some bungled Nazi business. He had never been punished. Then she said, 'Why are you here? What's he done now?'

'Do you know where he is?' said Willi.

'Last I heard, he was in Lindau,' she said.

'You haven't seen him?'

'I told you, I don't want anything to do with that shithead. He killed my Johann.'

Willi and Bergemann drove to Lindau. At the docks, they found the customs office. They went in and identified themselves to the customs official on duty. 'What can I do for you?' said the man.

'We're looking for Ernst Nutzke,' said Willi.

The man looked shocked at the question. 'Ernst Nutzke?' he said.

'That's right, Ernst Nutzke,' said Willi.

'He's dead,' said the official. 'Ernst Nutzke's dead.'

'Really?' said Willi. 'When did he die?'

'Last week. On Friday.'

'How did he die?' said Willi.

'He drowned,' said the man.

'Drowned?' said Bergemann.

'Yeah,' said the official. 'Funny, isn't it? All his life, he worked on the water, and he never learned to swim.'

Anna and Franzl

Ernst Nutzke had been found half in the water and half out beside one of the docks. Given his history with the black market and other criminal activity, his death was marked as suspicious. But an autopsy revealed that he had a high level of alcohol in his system and that he had in fact drowned. There were no injuries, internal or external, or other evidence of violence to his body. The police looked for clues of foul play but found none. The death was ruled an accident. Nutzke had been drunk, the dock was slippery from all the rain, and he had fallen in the water and drowned. As simple as that.

Willi and Bergemann drove back to Konstanz and delivered the few personal effects from his work locker to his sister. She wept at the news, called her brother a shithead again, and wanted to know how he had died. They told her.

It had happened to Willi before that some criminal had evaded prosecution by dying. He tried to think of it as a sort of justice, except it wasn't. Ernst Nutzke might have drowned even if he had been innocent of any wrongdoing. Outcomes like this were unsatisfactory to Willi, like a fault in the universe.

From Nutzke's sister, they went to the address Bobi had given Willi, where Anna and Franzl lived. The two-story yellow house might have been elegant eighty years earlier, but now it was a wreck. The small porch was collapsing, there was trash all around, windows were broken.

Bergemann waited in the car; Willi knocked on the door several times. He could hear a radio playing inside. After a while, a woman opened the door. She was drunk and held on to the door to keep from falling. 'Frau Brockel?' he said. He gave her his name. She just looked at him with empty eyes. He asked if he could see Anna and Franzl.

'They're busy,' said the woman.

'Busy?' said Willi. 'They're children.'

The woman shrugged her shoulders, turned, and staggered

back into the house, and Willi followed. There was a foul smell. Filthy furniture stood helter-skelter. There were clothes and empty bottles everywhere. The children were in the dusty backyard. It was littered with trash and more bottles. Anna and Franzl sat huddled together by a collapsing shed.

'See? They're busy,' said Frau Brockel.

'Frau Brockel, where is Herr Brockel?' said Willi.

Frau Brockel just shrugged and staggered back inside. Willi followed her into the kitchen. 'Is he here somewhere?' said Willi.

'No,' said Frau Brockel. 'He isn't here.'

'Where is he?'

'I don't know.'

'Is he living here?'

She looked Willi in the eye for the first time, and her face collapsed into anguish. Willi turned off the radio and looked around the kitchen to see whether there was any food. The sink was full of dirty dishes, pots, and pans.

'Frau Brockel, do you have any food?'

She opened a cupboard and pointed to a partial loaf of bread, a piece of cheese, a half-full bottle of milk, a few eggs, some wilted yellow celery, several potatoes that were sprouting.

'That's all you have? Are you eating?'

She nodded.

'And you're feeding Anna and Franzl?'

She nodded again.

'Do you have a telephone, Frau Brockel?'

She shook her head no.

Willi went out to the car and told Bergemann the situation, and Bergemann went to get someone from the Konstanz police. The police knew Herr Brockel. He had been in minor trouble off and on since coming back from Russia, wounded and severely alcoholic. 'He's probably drunk somewhere; he's a mean drunk, so it's better he's not home.'

Willi told Frau Brockel that he was taking Franzl and Anna with him to be reunited with their older brother, Bobi.

'Bobi?' she said, and her face lit up. 'How is Bobi?'

She showed Willi to the room where the children slept. To Willi's surprise, it was clean and pleasant. Pictures had been cut from magazines and tacked to the walls. Two small beds and two wardrobes had been painted blue and orange. Frau Brockel took little cardboard valises out of a cupboard and packed them with Franzl and Anna's few belongings. Then she gave Willi a ragged little stuffed rabbit that had once been blue. One of its button eyes was missing. 'Anna will want her Fufu,' she said.

Willi and Bergemann washed some pans and made an omelet and boiled potatoes, and sat with Frau Brockel, Franzl, and Anna while they ate. Frau Brockel explained to the children that they were going with the men, and they were going to live with Bobi. When they heard Bobi's name, they looked from Willi to Bergemann and back again, and the two men nodded. Willi said that was true, they were going to live with Bobi. And that Frau Brockel would visit them when she could. And Frau Brockel said yes, she would.

Anna sat in the backseat beside Willi. Franzl wanted to ride up front. Anna stared out of the side window, holding Fufu tightly. Franzl sat on the edge of the seat, watching Bergemann steering, braking, shifting gears. After a while, he asked Bergemann if he could drive, and Bergemann said no.

General Gehlen

M r West told his colleagues there would probably be no more trouble from Detective Geismeier. He had closed his case against Bernhard Pautsch. Pautsch had been sentenced to twenty years, and Geismeier would have been told by his superiors to move on to the next case.

It was true. Willi had been called to police headquarters along with Captain Breuer. They were shown into a large room where the Munich chief of detectives, an American colonel, and a dozen German and American civilians were sitting around a large conference table. There was paper and a pen in front of each man.

The chief of detectives spoke first and praised Willi for shutting down the trafficking ring and arresting the perpetrators. They had all been charged and were in prison, awaiting trial. The chief then read a commendation that, he said, would be inserted into Willi's record. He stood and walked over to where Willi stood and pinned a ribbon on his lapel.

He then made a little speech about how the new German police, hand in hand with the American military police – here he nodded in the direction of one of the American civilians who nodded back – must work to stem the rising tide of crime. He mentioned the illicit traffic in goods and money between West and East Germany. Willi couldn't help but think that the chief might be describing a Werner Krosius operation.

The chief then spoke of espionage, sabotage, and other subversive mischief coming from the East. The Russians were forging US dollars and circulating them in the West by way of Berlin. They were interfering with traffic between the West and Berlin through the Soviet Zone. The chief turned to Willi again. 'We need men like you on the front lines of our new Germany, Detective Geismeier. We police must keep our fledgling democracy on the straight and narrow, rebuilding Germany with the help of our American friends.' He paused and then spoke to the man sitting across the table from Willi. 'Would

you like to say a word about the great task facing us, General
Gehlen?'

General Gehlen, a German, wore a gray vested suit, a black
tie, and a white pocket square. He sat absolutely motionless
on his chair. He regarded Willi through tinted glasses with
unblinking eyes. He spoke in German. Willi could tell this was
a speech he had delivered many times.

There was no salutation, no preamble. *'Der Kommunismus!'*
he said. He expelled the word as though he were spitting out
something foul-tasting. 'Communism. That is the menace we
must focus on, and with a single, united mind. Communism must
be defeated by whatever means, whatever it may cost. The Soviet
Union is our enemy. Make no mistake. But we also now have
an enemy here' – he pointed downward for emphasis – 'here
within Germany. That enemy is the subversive fellow traveler,
that man or woman working day and night to infiltrate our ranks
with their totalitarian communist ideology. You can see them
everywhere – writing in some of our newspapers, playing on the
stages of our theaters, aspiring to join the ranks of government.
They say they are well intentioned; they say they are striving for
equality and social justice. But make no mistake: they are not.

'They call themselves "social democrats" or "socialists," but
these people are as dangerous as the communists themselves.
Because to the communists, they are the tools, the instruments,
the means to a communist end, which is the establishment of a
Soviet communist regime in Germany and around the world.
They and their alien socialist ideology must be defeated and
banished from society.

'Now, some of the people on our side in this life-and-death
struggle may have committed errors in the past. They may be
less perfect than we would wish. That is of no importance. In
this war against the communist evil, every ally is essential to our
success. We must make use of all the means at our disposal if
we are going to win. And we *must* win. We have no choice. This
is nothing less than all-out war.

'Detective Geismeier,' he said. 'Whatever past infractions you
seek to rectify, whatever axes you may have to grind, they are
of no importance. Not while our crusade against the communists
is being fought, not until it is won. Either you are a part of this

effort, either you are with us, or you are against us. Everyone must understand that by now. And those who do not, those who insist on going a different way, will be crushed beneath the wheels of history.'

Gehlen stopped speaking. The room remained silent. After a moment, Gehlen stood and left the room, followed by the two men who had sat to his left and right. Willi guessed they were former SS. The chief of detectives looked over at one of the Americans who gave him a little nod. 'You're dismissed, Captain, Detective,' he said.

Willi and Breuer stood and saluted. They drove back to the fifth precinct headquarters in silence.

It seemed remarkable to Willi that a German general could not only have maintained his rank but also have landed an obviously important job in the new government. Willi had heard of General Gehlen during the war but couldn't place him. A little asking around revealed that Major General Reinhard Gehlen had been Hitler's head of intelligence on the eastern front. Willi guessed Gehlen had used whatever he had learned about the Soviet army to make a deal with the Americans. In fact, Gehlen had been stockpiling intelligence on the Soviets for his own purposes long before the war ended. He and his lieutenants had buried fifty-two steel drums filled with intelligence documents and microfilm in a secret location. Then Gehlen surrendered to the Americans and offered this treasure trove in exchange for immunity from prosecution.

For the Americans, Gehlen was a gift from heaven. He knew *everything* about the Soviets, and anti-communism was his religion. There was no question of prosecution. American military intelligence helped him set up his own independent spy organization. They gave him money, lots of money. They gave him free rein to recruit dozens of former Nazi officers for his new organization. Eventually, the Gehlen Organization became closely associated with the CIA and evolved into the new Federal Republic of Germany's own Federal Intelligence Service. Gehlen was promoted to lieutenant general in the Bundeswehr, the army of the Federal Republic of Germany.

Werner Krosius had met Gehlen earlier when he was plundering the Russian battlefield for arms. And through the Americans, they had now reconnected. Gehlen saw right away how useful Krosius might be in defeating communism. Krosius had a new clean identity, a 'legitimate' business, money and connections in both East and West Germany, and a willingness to do whatever needed to be done. He was that less-than-perfect ally Gehlen had just lectured Willi about.

Willi met Bergemann for a walk through the English Garden. A pair of ducks were swimming across the pond with a string of ducklings in tow. Like Willi, Bergemann had heard of Gehlen but didn't know much. He had lots of questions, to which Willi didn't have the answers yet. But he was pretty sure about the connection between Gehlen and Krosius. 'Gehlen as good as told me,' said Willi. 'But I think he's making a big mistake.'

'A big mistake?'

'Trusting Krosius.' Willi didn't have any trouble imagining Krosius as a double or even a triple agent, betraying each side to the other. That was the way he had always operated. And there was money in it.

The Currency Exchange

Since the mid-nineteenth century, before the town of Köpenik had been incorporated into the city of Berlin, the Director General's secretary Gerda Drechsler's family had owned a grand manor house in the center of that town. Gerda's mother had recently died and now the house stood empty.

Gerda went to Köpenik for the funeral, wept for her mother, and went by to see the family home. Standing in front of it, among the great sycamores that towered over the place, she decided she wanted to hold on to the house, even as the Russians were confiscating all private properties. The odds were against her, but she sought out the Russian Major Valensky who was in charge of the confiscation operation in Köpenik anyway.

She found Valensky in a local bar throwing back shots of vodka. Gerda had once been a professional seductress, so the major was no match for her. After they had spent a few hours in a room upstairs, the major was more than willing to allow her to continue to own the family home, at least for the time being, in exchange for her favors.

In the course of their relationship, Gerda learned that the major, the son of the great Soviet hero General Valensky, was also an aspiring capitalist. He ran what he called a 'currency exchange.' At the moment, he had a hundred thousand US dollars at his disposal. He said it was Marshall Plan money that had gone astray, as money easily did these days, and he proposed exchanging it for Reichsmarks which would obviously be of more use to him than US dollars.

Gerda told her boss the Director General about the major's idea. The Director General knew from General Gehlen himself that one of his schemes was to flood the Soviet Zone with counterfeit Reichsmarks. He saw that he could both please General Gehlen and make a nice killing for himself by trading the major counterfeit Reichsmarks for his dollars.

'Arrange a meeting,' he told Gerda.

'Will you be notifying General Gehlen of this . . . project?' she said.

'I think it's better we don't,' he said. Werner Krosius's felonious heart still beat beneath the blue serge suit of the Director General of Allied Development, GmbH.

Around midnight on a warm April night, the Director General drove his Mercedes into East Berlin, crossing at the Karl-Marxstraße and then driving east in the direction of Köpenick. He had not seen whether he was being followed, but he was pretty sure he was. You always were these days. This was Berlin.

The division between West and East was not quite a year old, and yet the differences were already stark. While the West featured lively commerce and construction cranes everywhere, and bright lights and traffic, the East was desolate. The shells of bombed and useless buildings lined the streets. The few shops had mostly empty shelves, which didn't matter since people didn't have money anyway. Electricity was intermittent. Streets were unlit and empty of life. The only vehicles you saw were a few official cars and Russian military vehicles on the prowl.

In Köpenick, the Director General found the warehouse just where the Wendenschloßstraße crossed the Spree. A Russian jeep was parked by the door. A dim light was barely visible through the window. The Director General parked facing the jeep. He took the Luger from under the seat, tucked it into his belt, and buttoned his jacket over it. He got out of the car and knocked on the door. Hearing nothing, he turned the knob and went inside.

A car drove slowly up to the building. It stopped. A flashbulb flashed, and the car drove off slowly across the bridge.

After a half-hour, the Director General came out of the warehouse, got in his car, turned around, and drove back the way he had come.

It did not take long for Major Valensky to discover that the Reichsmarks the Director General had delivered were forgeries. At first, he was furious, but then he had to laugh when he remembered that the dollars he had traded for them were forgeries, too.

The dollars were better forgeries than the Reichsmarks. Even after the Director General learned they were forgeries, he was able to dispose of them in a way that turned a nice profit. He didn't tell Gerda he had been tricked. And neither did Major Valensky.

Meanwhile, with Bergemann's help, Willi had found the documents of incorporation of Allied Development, GmbH. They were signed by Georg Berghof and Lukas Pettermann. He found the telephone number and address for Allied Development. It would be easy enough to learn whether Berghof and Krosius were one and the same person. All he had to do was call the number and ask for Krosius, and Mr West, whose minions would be listening in, would do the rest.

The Crazy Detective

Willi asked the Director General's secretary whether he could speak to Werner Krosius. Gerda kept her cool and said there was no one there by that name. Willi said, 'Well, would you please ask him to call me when he comes in?' He gave his name and number, and asked her to read the number back to him.

Willi heard in a matter of hours from Captain Breuer. He could tell right away that Werner Krosius was definitely Georg Berghof. 'God dammit, Geismeier,' said Breuer. 'What is wrong with you?' It was a rhetorical question.

Things did not go any better when he got to Breuer's office. The captain had heard from Mr West that Geismeier had undermined an important anti-communist operation, all for nothing. Geismeier had been warned, and he had failed to heed the warning. Now he had placed his own career in jeopardy, Captain Breuer's career as well, and there were serious discussions at the highest levels about whether Geismeier shouldn't be charged with various crimes including treason.

'God dammit, Geismeier,' said Breuer again, sputtering in frustration. 'I suggest you get yourself a good criminal lawyer.'

'Yes, sir,' said Willi.

Lukas Pettermann was startled when Willi called him. He hung up on Willi.

Willi had made it clear to everyone that he was obsessed and was not going to give up. Pettermann called Mr West. 'That crazy bastard is going to go to Berlin.'

'Well, let that son of a bitch try,' said Mr West. 'Agents are in place. We'll arrest the son of a bitch if he gets anywhere near Krosius. Shit, I'll arrest him if he comes anywhere near Berlin!'

In fact, there was very little Willi could do to Krosius within the law. Captain Breuer was right. Mr West was right. Willi had already wildly exceeded his jurisdiction as a Munich police detective. Furthermore, Krosius's culpability in the murder of Captain Charlie Herder and Fedor Blaskowitz was from another era. It was a historical artifact, and it was a tenuous fact at best. And when it came to the sexual exploitation of children, Krosius was three steps removed from that actual crime. In fact, most of Krosius's criminality, at least that which Willi knew about or suspected, seemed to pass for normal behavior these days. Willi, they said, was acting like an avenging angel, not like a policeman.

'Let it go,' said Bergemann.

'You're crazy,' said Lola. 'You have three children in your care now,' she said. 'That's reality. Not this other stuff. Krosius, the war – that's a nightmare that's behind us. It's over.'

'I know you're right, but I don't know if I can let it go,' said Willi. But he wrote a letter to the chief of detectives anyway.

May 4, 1946

Sir,

I hereby submit my resignation from the Munich Police Department.

Respectfully,

Willi Geismeier.

Willi folded the paper in thirds, put it in an envelope, and addressed it to the Munich chief of detectives. He put the envelope in his inside jacket pocket and left for work.

There was plenty of criminal activity that had nothing to do with the war or Werner Krosius. A string of small robberies crossed his desk, and he set about finding out who was doing them. He carried the envelope with him. It weighed nothing, and yet he felt the great weight of it as he went about his business.

Willi had a dream one night in which he found himself wading through a sea of ferns in a dark and unfamiliar forest. He sensed that there were animals scurrying around below him. The ferns rustled and waved as they moved here and there, and he heard them snorting and snuffling and smelled their strong odor. He tried to touch them, to see what they were, but they eluded him.

Then he found himself in a dark, murky pond, and it too was filled with beasts he could only sense. Sometimes he saw their dark backs break the surface of the brown water. And then suddenly the water drained from the pond, and the beasts, whatever they were, were gone, and clean fresh water flowed in. And floating toward him was the little girl Anna, holding up Fufu and smiling.

Family Life

Willi had not only violated police procedures; he had interfered with the work of the American occupation. High American intelligence officials, by way of Mr West, insisted that Willi should be charged with espionage or anything else that would land him in prison for a long time. General Gehlen also let it be known that Detective Geismeier should be made an example of, to warn any other policeman or public servant who decided his career was more important than defeating the communists. Willi was suspended without pay while they decided what the charges would be.

'Pappi!' said Anna. She ran up to Willi. She was always the first child up in the morning. Willi put his arms around the little girl. Willi and Lola had had their coffee. It was real coffee, a gift from Lieutenant O'Connor, the US military policeman that had first hired Willi back into the Munich police force. He and Willi had become friends. 'You're one crazy son of a bitch, Geismeier,' he said. 'I admire that.'

The little girl climbed on to her chair. Lola warmed some milk, poured it into a cup, put just enough coffee in to make it brown, and gave it to Anna. Anna spread jam on a piece of black bread, getting more jam on her bread than on her fingers, which was progress. She took a big bite. Franzl and Bobi came in one after the other.

After breakfast, Willi took Anna and Franzl for a walk. A path had been cleared so that you could cross the damaged rail yards, and someone had planted birch saplings here and there along the way. Their early leaves were the finest pale green. Anna was in a hurry to get to the forest, but Franzl wanted to look at the freight cars lying across the tracks, and Willi explained that was where the bombs had thrown them.

The forest had been bombed, too. Trees were splintered, and there were craters filled with water thanks to all the rain they had had. But some trees had survived, and there was new growth as well. And everything that was still alive had leaves in different shades of green, all of it new and tender. They stayed on the marked paths because there were unexploded bombs. Some areas had been marked with yellow or orange tape.

An elderly man and his dog coming toward them stopped while the man attached a lead to the dog. '*Grüß Gott!*' said the man.

'*Grüß Gott!*' said Willi, and Franzl and Anna repeated the greeting.

'He's friendly,' said the man, pointing at his dog.

Willi smiled, but he had already told the children they shouldn't pet a dog they didn't know. Plenty of people have been bitten by friendly dogs.

Bobi hadn't come with them because he thought he was too old to take walks. Besides, he had a job. Really. People didn't believe it when he said so. But Willi's old friend Gerd Fegelein was back from wherever he had been during the war, and Lerchenau Bicycles was back in business in the old place, a twenty-minute bicycle ride from the Geismeier warehouse. Fegelein had offered to take Bobi on as an apprentice and teach him the trade.

'The trade?' said Willi.

'Bicycle mechanics,' said Fegelein with a laugh. His trade when he was younger had been cat burglar, but all that was long ago.

Bobi worked at Lerchenau Bicycles most Saturdays. He liked bicycles, liked having a job, liked Fegelein. As it happened, Bobi liked learning, too. He had been out of school for several years and at first had refused to go back. Willi and Lola said he had to, and he eventually agreed. He was put in a class with mostly nine-year-olds, which made him feel stupid since he was so much older. But Willi sat with him while he did his homework and saw how smart he was. Willi had started speaking to him in English sometimes, and it turned out Bobi had a knack for that as well. 'You'll be with kids your own age before you know it,' said Willi, 'and then you'll leave them behind, too. I promise.'

And that turned out to be true.

Dead Again

One Monday morning, Willi's telephone rang. It was Pettermann, the lawyer. 'Director General Berghof is dead,' he said.

'Who?' said Willi, taken by surprise. He hadn't spoken to or heard from Pettermann for several months.

'Krosius. Krosius is dead,' said Pettermann.

'What? Again?' said Willi.

'No. He's really dead.' According to Pettermann, the man known to many as Director General Georg Berghof had been pulled from the Spree River one morning the previous week. His Mercedes had been parked nearby with the key in the ignition. Pettermann didn't know any more than that.

Willi went to the precinct and knocked on the captain's door. At first, Captain Breuer refused to even see him. Willi went in anyway. Breuer told him to get the hell out of his office.

'Captain,' said Willi, 'I have a letter of resignation here.' He pulled the envelope halfway out of his pocket so the captain could see it.

'All right,' said the captain. 'Give it here.' He held out his hand.

'I'll give it to you,' said Willi, 'if you give me permission to go to Berlin.'

'Berlin?'

'Krosius is dead, Captain. I want to see the body.'

'You're out of your mind, Geismeier. Get out of here.'

'Captain Breuer, I'll go with your permission or without it. If I go with your permission, I'll hand you my resignation when I get back, and you'll be rid of me. Without your permission – well, the mess I'm going to make I'll leave to your imagination.'

'Hell, no!' said Mr West when he heard what Willi meant to do. 'That man is a fucking lunatic and a menace.' But General Gehlen liked the idea of having Geismeier turning over rocks while under their surveillance. 'He'll reveal his contacts and

connections in both East and West. A whole collection of communists and fellow travelers.' Gehlen had a vivid imagination. Mr
West still thought it was a crazy idea, but after reflecting, he
didn't see how it could do any real harm. And he liked humoring
Gehlen. And who knew, it might even turn out to be useful.
Maybe that son of a bitch Geismeier would finally do something
to get himself arrested and charged. So Willi was given permission to make the trip.

An American agent followed Willi on to the night train to
Berlin. Willi spotted him a few rows back, pretending to read a
newspaper. The train was full. The cars swayed gently, and soon
the lights dimmed and the sound of deep breathing and occasional
snores could be heard, including from the agent and then Willi.
Only one young man in the entire car remained awake, a student
returning to university to take exams.

A different agent followed Willi on to the S-Bahn. He called
into General Gehlen's office to report that the subject was at a
West Berlin police precinct headquarters. Gehlen was disappointed when he got the report but said the agent should stay
with him.

Willi knew he was being followed and made no effort to lose
the agent, since nothing he was doing or was going to do was
outside normal police protocol. Detective Detlev Waldborn had
been assigned to brief Willi and show him whatever he wanted
to see connected with the Director General's death – within
reason, of course. Willi could tell that Waldborn had been briefed
about him and his sinister and subversive ways. The young detective seemed uneasy, as though he were in a cage with a gorilla.
The gorilla might seem docile, even friendly. But he could go
crazy at any minute.

Willi wanted to see the body, and Waldborn took him to the
coroner's office. It was nearby so they walked. In the morgue,
the coroner pulled out the drawer. Werner Krosius, even with a
large gash above his left eye, looked to be at peace.

'Is that what killed him?' said Willi, pointing at the gash.

'No,' said the coroner. 'He drowned.'

'Did the wound on his head cause him to go into the water?'

'I don't know,' said the coroner. 'He could have hit his head
when he went in, although we didn't find any evidence of that.'

'Can you tell what made the wound?'

'No. We didn't find anything.'

'Can you tell if it was blunt or sharp?'

'I'd say blunt,' said the coroner. 'But there was nothing in or around the wound that tells me any more than that.'

'No concrete, splinters, nothing like that?'

'Nothing.'

'And there were no other injuries?'

'None that I found.'

'And when you opened him up?'

'Nothing out of the ordinary. Everything looked normal.'

'Do you have his clothes and belongings?'

'I have them,' said Waldborn. 'They're back at the office.'

Willi and Waldborn walked back and chatted a bit as they walked, about life in Berlin, about the work. Willi said he needed some coffee. He hadn't slept that well on the train. They stopped in a café. He bought Waldborn a coffee, too.

Waldborn thought Willi seemed like a nice guy and a conscientious detective. He was impressed he had come all this way to close out a case. He wondered what Willi might have done to get the whole American and German intelligence establishment on his neck.

'I just get under their skin,' said Willi with a smile and a shrug.

'Georg Berghof seems to have been a mysterious character,' said Waldborn, trying a different angle. 'I'm not supposed to ask you about that.'

'But you're asking,' said Willi.

'Yes,' said Waldborn.

'His real name was Werner Krosius,' said Willi. 'He was not the director general of anything. He's a gangster from way back. I'd better not say any more than that. It could cause you problems.'

'Really?' said Waldborn. 'How?'

'Knowing all this is what got me in trouble,' said Willi.

Waldborn chewed that over for a while. Then he nodded his head. 'OK. Thanks,' he said. Then: 'Do they think you killed him?'

'I don't think so,' said Willi.

'Did you?' said Waldborn.

'No,' said Willi. 'I wanted Krosius arrested and brought to trial. Anyway, I was in Munich at the time of the murder.'

Something about Waldborn reminded Willi of his younger self.

Willi explained to Waldborn that he had been part of the so-called Flower Gang during the war, a diverse and sizable group of underground operators, many of whom were unknown to him, most of whom would have wanted Krosius killed if they had known who he was. He didn't think Krosius's complicity with the SS and Gestapo was well known, but he couldn't be sure of that either.

Back at the office, Waldborn got the box for the Berghof case out of the evidence room. Inside was a leather briefcase. It had been in the front seat of the car and had been filled with counterfeit German money. There were three passports – one German, one American, one Russian – all for Georg Berghof. The American passport had stamps indicating it had been used in Washington, New York, London, Istanbul, and Paris. The Russian and German passports had no stamps at all. There was always the chance the passports were fake. Willi made notes. There was a wallet with a little cash, a driving license, several club membership cards that Willi also noted. There was a plastic bag with coins, an expensive watch, a set of keys, a handkerchief. Something blue at the bottom of the bag caught his eye.

'Is that a piece of yarn?' he said.

'Yeah,' said Waldborn.

'Was that in his pocket?'

'No,' said Waldborn. 'It was tied around his wrist.'

Willi put it back in the plastic bag.

'Some sort of amulet, I guess,' said Waldborn.

Finding Ernst

Elke had never let go of the thought that the killer Ernst had been a border guard. She had gone back to the border again and again. She would study the agents through binoculars, watch the shifts change, but never saw Ernst or anyone who resembled him. She looked for the other men that had been there that day. But she didn't remember them at all, so she couldn't know.

One day, a customs agent came to the pool. He was in uniform; he had just finished his shift. Elke signed him in, gave him a towel and a locker key. He was studying her, then it clicked. 'Die Laterne,' he said. 'You were the singer there, weren't you?'

'Yes,' said Elke. 'Long ago.'

'You were good. I liked the whole band, but you were really good. I remember you singing "I'll Be Seeing You" and "Beyond the Blue Horizon." I really liked your singing.'

'Thank you,' she said. 'That's very nice. Do you know someone in customs or on the border named Ernst?

The abrupt switch surprised the man a little, but he gave it some thought. 'There's a guy, Ernst Nutzke. Is that the guy?'

'I don't know,' said Elke. 'What's he like?'

'I don't know him,' said the man, 'but I know about him. I don't know if he's still in the service. Do you know him?'

'No, not really,' said Elke.

Norbert Wolff the agent came back again a few days later. Elke checked him in again. 'Ernst Nutzke's still in the service,' he told her. 'He's a crook. I don't know how he's still there. He must have some connections. He's in Lindau, the night shift. From what I hear, he's a dangerous character.'

The next time Norbert came to swim, he offered to help Elke with whatever she had with Nutzke, if he could. She said he couldn't really help. All right, he said, but if she ever needed his help . . . In the meantime, would she like to have dinner with him? Elke said she'd think about it.

She went to the pool and watched him swim for a couple of

laps. He swam with smooth, strong, steady strokes, his kick hardly splashing. Back and forth he went with a visible serenity. When he came to turn in his towel and locker key, she said she would like to have dinner with him.

'Saturday?' he said.

'I work weekends,' she said.

'Tuesday?' he said.

'Tuesday is good,' she said.

'I'm learning to cook,' he said. 'I'm studying to be a chef. How about if you come to my apartment? I'll make us a nice supper.'

The next afternoon, Elke took the ferry to the island town of Lindau before the shifts changed at the customs office. She hid inside a ruined shed across from the office and watched through the small, dirty window. The shift started at nine. Nutzke was the first to arrive. He went into the office. Three more border patrol agents arrived and checked in. After a while, they all came out. The other three left; their posts were elsewhere. But Nutzke remained behind; his patrol began right there.

Elke had intended just to find out where Nutzke was and pass it on to Willi. Then the police would come and arrest Nutzke, and justice would be done. Now, though, she thought if she could observe Nutzke during his shift, she would have that much more information for the police.

She watched as Nutzke strapped a pistol and holster around his waist. Then he suddenly stepped up to the window where she was watching. She stepped back, afraid he'd see her, afraid he'd hear her heart pounding. Her heel hit something, and it made a noise, but he didn't hear it. He just studied his reflection, peeled his lips back, and looked at his ugly teeth. Ernst tugged his uniform cap further down on his forehead, took one final look, and turned to go.

The docks near the office were anywhere from ten to twenty meters apart and connected by wooden gangways along the shore. The gangway went for about two hundred meters, then there was an earthen path for several hundred meters. Boats were tied up along the docks – small ferries, fishing boats, pleasure boats – but there was no one around.

Nutzke set off along the gangway past the first dock. A few

lamps on posts cast circles of dim light along the gangway every so often. When Ernst left the light in front of the office, he disappeared into the darkness only to emerge further along the way under the next lamp.

Elke came out of the shed and followed him. She could slip around the edges of the light-islands and that way remain nearly invisible. Nutzke limped along slowly. Elke tried to stay fifty meters back. When he got to a pier, he walked out, shining his light on to the boats tied up there, although he didn't go out on to every pier.

Elke waited for him to emerge into the light before moving ahead. That way she could see where he was looking before moving ahead herself. After a while, she realized she didn't know how far his patrol would take him, and if he turned to come back, he would then be facing her. She decided to turn now while he was still walking away. She was in the dark, but at that moment, for whatever reason, Nutzke turned to look out along the dock beside him and caught a glimpse of her out of the corner of his eye.

He began walking toward her, then broke into a sort of gallop. She ducked down beside a small boat, but he had seen her. He was faster than she could have imagined. In a second, he was in front of her, and in the dim light she saw the expression of recognition cross his face. 'You!' he shouted and reached out for her with both hands. She dodged him and ran to the end of the short dock, with him one step behind her. He was so close she heard his breathing, smelled the alcohol on his breath. He got his arm around her neck at the end of the dock. They teetered back and forth there as she struggled to get away. Then they went over the edge and plunged into the black water.

Ernst now grabbed her with both arms, trying to save himself. He gasped and screamed and took in water as he did. He thrashed and tried to climb up Elke. And Elke, to save herself, went deeper and deeper until finally, but slowly, he let go. He hung there in the water, lifeless. She pushed him away, kicked her way to the surface, and took in air. Then she found him again and dragged him to a sloping bit of shore. She crawled out and, with her last strength, pulled him on to shore as far as she could, so he was at least partly on land.

She lay there gasping for air for a while. Then she turned him on his front and pushed on his back with both hands. She pushed rhythmically, again and again, for a long time. Some water came out of his nose and mouth, but not enough. He was dead.

She sat there for a while, her arms around her knees. She rocked back and forth. It wasn't very cold, but she shivered. She looked at him for a long time. Then she reached into her pocket and took a small coil of the blue yarn she had carried in her pocket since . . . then. She broke off a length of yarn and tied it around Ernst's dead wrist.

Willi in Lindau

The press had somehow got wind of Director General Berghof's death. Although he was not well known, just being the head of a company made him a notable person. The press wanted more information. The Americans issued a press release stating that Georg Berghof had spent the evening consummating a big development deal. On his way home, he had suffered a massive heart attack and had died.

The West German papers published a brief summary of Berghof's life, based on a second press release and all of it entirely untrue. The East German papers sensed there was something fishy about the story and mostly ignored it. Only the *Berliner Zeitung* had an editorial that mentioned Berghof's sudden death as a cautionary tale about the corrupt and tragic practices of a capitalist society.

Detective Waldborn had interviewed everyone known to have had contact with Berghof, including his secretary, Gerda Drechsler. She could tell interesting stories about Werner Krosius but knew very little about his life as the Director General. Waldborn's conversation with Willi hadn't been particularly illuminating either, except to reveal that there were probably a lot of people that wanted Berghof dead.

Aside from his clandestine and criminal contacts, the Director General had had very little to do with anyone. The consensus opinion among those actually in the know in the West – General Gehlen, Mr West, and the higher-ups in the American intelligence hierarchy – was that Werner Krosius had been assassinated by the Soviets because of the work he was doing for the Americans to disrupt the East German economy. Meanwhile, the East German and Soviet secret services believed Director General Georg Berghof had been assassinated by the Americans because of work he had been doing for the Soviets to disrupt the West German economy. The contradictory versions of his life and death all but guaranteed that the true story would never come out.

After his visit to Berlin, Willi had taken a train back to Munich, still followed by one of General Gehlen's agents. He arrived home late in the evening. Franzl and Anna were sound asleep. Bobi was sitting under a lamp, reading.

Lola had made a salad, and she and Willi had a late supper. She told him about taking the children to the zoo. It had been badly bombed during the war. A lot of the animals had been killed, but it was open again in a sort of provisional way. Willi told her about Berlin, about the young detective Detlev Waldborn, about how the dead Director General really was Werner Krosius. He told her about everything except the blue yarn.

He helped her clean up and wash the dishes. He looked around the apartment, which was somewhat improvised, being in the corner of an old warehouse. From where he stood, he could see into the living room with rugs on the floor and pictures on the walls. He saw the doors to the children's bedroom, to his and Lola's bedroom. He saw Bobi now asleep on the chair. The book had slid off on to the floor. He saw the life ahead of them in his mind's eye.

Lola studied him for a moment, figured out that something was going on, and let it be. She motioned with her head toward Bobi. Willi went over and picked him up and walked him to his bed.

Willi understood that he and Bergemann had accepted the explanation of Ernst Nutzke's death as accidental too easily. The next day, Willi drove to Lindau. He went alone. He drove at a reasonable speed and used the brakes as they were meant to be used. He thought it must be the children that had that effect on him. At the Lindau police station, he introduced himself and asked to see the evidence box for Nutzke's death. There was very little in it. His clothes, a plastic bag with a fancy wristwatch, the contents of his pockets, including house keys, some coins, a pocket calendar with names and numbers. Willi turned the pages back and forth.

'We're still working on some of that,' said the desk officer with a wave of his hand. 'Nutzke was pretty big in the black market. We're checking it all out.' He held out his hand, and Willi gave it back. There was no blue yarn.

Willi asked to speak to the policeman who had overseen the investigation of Nutzke's death. 'That would be me,' said the desk sergeant. Willi looked at him with raised eyebrows. 'We're a small town,' said the sergeant, 'and we're short-handed.'

Willi nodded and smiled. 'Of course,' he said. 'Who was the first officer on the scene?'

The desk sergeant smiled. 'That would be me as well.'

Willi asked him who had found and reported the body, how the body had been dealt with, who had had access to it, how it had been transported to the coroner, whether Nutzke had been wearing any jewelry or other ornaments, whether the coroner had reported anything unusual – every question Willi could think of where blue yarn might have been the answer. Finally, Willi asked straight out whether there had been a piece of blue yarn on his arm or anywhere else on his body.

The answer was no. The desk officer had followed protocol and had been very thorough, but there was no blue yarn.

'Did you know Ernst Nutzke at all?' said Willi.

'I arrested him a few times. Once for black-market dealing, which his lawyer got him out of. And twice for disorderly conduct. He was a brawler, Detective, a nasty piece of work. I don't know how he managed to stay a border agent. Connections, I guess.'

'I guess,' said Willi. 'Do you remember who his lawyer might have been?'

'I could look it up.' He got up and went to a filing cabinet where he rummaged around for a minute. 'Pettermann. Lukas Pettermann, with offices in Munich and Berlin.'

'Thank you,' said Willi.

'Anything else I can do for you, Detective?'

'No, thank you, Officer. Thanks for your excellent information.'

'We're a small precinct, Detective, but we pride ourselves on doing everything by the book.'

Willi asked where the body had been found and went there to look around. The customs agent on duty showed him exactly where it had been. He asked the customs agent the same questions about the blue yarn and got the same answers. He prowled around on the rocky shore for a half-hour, looking here and there, thinking the yarn might have been snagged on a rock, caught on a nearby pier. But too much time had passed, and even if he found something now, it would be entirely inconclusive.

The Swimmer

Norbert Wolff bought a decent Italian red wine. He bought a nice brown trout from a fisherman at his lakeside stand. He got a chicken and some tomatoes from his mother's farm. He had to do a real search to find a few threads of saffron. His paella turned out nicely.

At nine o'clock, Elke still hadn't showed up. This was not like her. If she didn't come, something had happened. He blew out the candles and went to find her. She was not at home. He knocked at the door at the pool. Herr Luthi said, yes, she was there. *Still* there, he said. She had been swimming for a long time, over an hour, back and forth, back and forth.

Norbert found her dressed. She was folding and stacking towels. She had a hard time meeting his eyes. She didn't want to be touched. So he sat down and waited.

Little by little, in response to his careful questions, she told him about following Nutzke, being seen, then being attacked.

'He couldn't swim,' she said. 'That son of a bitch couldn't swim.'

'It was an accident,' he said.

'It was an accident that I caused,' she said. Norbert took her home. He reheated the paella and they ate it without the candlelight.

'Why Nutzke?' he asked finally. 'Why were you following him?'

'I was called Clover,' she said.

'Clover?' he said.

'The name I went by during the war,' she said. By the next morning, he knew more or less the whole story.

Elke knew that Detective Geismeier would eventually find out that Ernst Nutzke was the killer the SS had hired. And he would eventually find out Nutzke was dead. Norbert persuaded her that she should go to Munich and seek the detective out. He said he'd go with her. But before they could go, Willi showed up.

Norbert had met Elke at the pool, and they were walking home together, and suddenly Willi was there walking beside them. Willi gave Elke his hand, and then Norbert. Willi walked to Norbert's home with them, and they invited him in.

Willi asked Elke how she was doing, what she was doing. She said she was fine. She said she was working at the municipal pool. She had become an enthusiastic swimmer since the war, she said, and swam every night after work. Willi said he knew that and it was part of what he wanted to talk to her about.

Norbert stood to leave the room, but Elke said she wanted him to stay. Willi said he had no objection, and Norbert sat down again. Then Elke told Willi the whole story, just as she had told it to Norbert, starting with her search for Nutzke and ending with tying yarn around Nutzke's wrist. She described how his wrist was cold and hard and heavy and turning blue itself, and how she had wrapped the yarn around it twice and tied a knot, and then let the dead hand drop on to the stones.

She said how she hated Nutzke for killing Charlie and Geranium, and how she wanted him to be punished but not to kill him. Her intention had been to learn as much about Ernst Nutzke as she could and then to pass everything she learned on to Willi.

'Why did you tie the yarn around his wrist?' said Willi.

Elke said, 'That's how you knew it was me, isn't it? It was a stupid thing to do. I always carried blue yarn with me, a kind of remembrance. I think I just wanted to mark the way, if you know what I mean. Like we did back then. That I – someone – knew who he really was.'

'Do you know who Werner Krosius is?' said Willi.

'No, I don't think so.' said Elke. 'Who is he?'

Willi had the drawing Joachim Ballitz had made and showed it to Elke.

'Oh. Joachim did a drawing like that for me, too. But I never saw the guy or even found out who he was. Is that Werner Krosius?'

'Yes,' said Willi.

'Who is he?' said Elke.

'He was a black marketeer and a Nazi collaborator. He worked with the SS. He's the one that found and hired Ernst Nutzke.'

'Where is he?' said Elke.

'He recently drowned in the Spree River in Berlin.'

Elke looked at Willi with wide eyes. She looked at Norbert. She didn't say anything.

'When he was pulled out of the water, he had a piece of blue yarn around his wrist.'

'In Berlin?' said Elke.

'Yes,' said Willi.

'And you think it was me.'

'I'm asking,' said Willi.

'It wasn't me,' said Elke. 'I've never even been to Berlin. When was it?'

'Last week on Tuesday evening, the fifteenth.'

Elke said that was her day off, but she had worked Monday and Wednesday evening.

Willi asked whether she had seen anyone between Monday and Wednesday evening.

She said she hadn't.

'So, it wouldn't have been easy, but you could have gotten to Berlin and back. Plus, his death resembles Nutzke's: the manner of his death, your motives, and most particularly the blue yarn.'

'Except, I didn't do it,' said Elke. 'I killed Nutzke; I didn't kill what's-his-name.'

'Krosius,' said Willi. 'Werner Krosius. These days he went by Director General Georg Berghof.'

'I never heard of him. I didn't kill him,' said Elke. 'Are you going to arrest me?'

'No,' said Willi.

'Why not?' said Elke.

'Because I don't have any evidence that you did it,' said Willi.

'Do you think I did it?' said Elke.

'I don't know,' said Willi. 'But I don't think so.'

'Why not?' said Elke.

Willi replied with a question of his own. 'Why didn't you report Nutzke's attack and his drowning to the police?'

Elke looked at Norbert. 'You said the same thing,' she said. 'I didn't report it because I knew how it would look,' she said to Willi. 'How it looks,' she corrected herself.

'Who else have you told about this?' said Willi.

'No one,' said Elke.

'And you?' said Willi, looking at Norbert.

'I haven't told anyone,' said Norbert.

'Don't either of you tell anyone,' said Willi. 'No one. Not now, not ever.'

He stood to leave. Elke and Norbert stood, too. 'One more thing,' said Willi. 'The blue yarn on Nutzke's arm . . . it was never found.'

'What do you mean?' said Elke.

'As far as the police or anyone else is concerned, there was no blue yarn. After learning Krosius had blue yarn on his arm, I went to the police in Lindau to see whether there was blue yarn on Nutzke's arm or anywhere at the site. It wasn't in their report, it wasn't among the evidence. I went to the site. It wasn't there. I went to Nutzke's sister. She had all his personal belongings the police had collected, still in the box. No blue yarn anywhere. The only way I know there was a blue yarn is because you just told me. There's no blue yarn. There's no evidence you were there that night.'

'What happened to it?' said Elke.

'I don't know. Torn off maybe when the body was moved? Came apart from being in the water? Who knows? Maybe it was carried off by a crow and woven into her nest. The fact remains: it's gone. It's as though it was never there.'

The Resignation

Everyone had their theories. Mr West believed Werner Krosius had cheated the Russian major out of a lot of money, and that had probably got him killed.

'Maybe that's part of it,' said General Gehlen, 'but that's not the whole story.'

'So you think he was a double agent?' said Mr West.

'I *know* he was a double agent,' said the general. 'And somebody blew his cover.'

'Are you thinking it's that detective – Geismeier?' said Mr West.

Gehlen had a look on his face as though he had just eaten something rotten. 'Maybe,' he said. He remembered then that operatives had been tailing Geismeier. He sent an assistant to get the latest surveillance reports. The reports contained only what seemed like official police business or ordinary activity. The phone numbers were police numbers or personal. Oh, and there was a weekend trip to Lindau.

'Where's Lindau?' said Mr West.

'Down by Switzerland,' said Gehlen's assistant.

'Very pretty,' said General Gehlen.

'So no contacts in Berlin, no contacts with the East,' said Mr West.

'None that we know of,' said the general.

'So we're barking up the wrong tree,' said West.

'I'm afraid so,' said the general.

Both men still wanted to arrest Willi Geismeier. But he had been in Munich the night of the murder, so he had not killed Werner Krosius, and his earlier interference had been nothing more than a nuisance. General Gehlen decided it might be a good idea to keep a tail on him. Maybe something will turn up.

'What's this?' said Captain Breuer when Willi handed him an envelope, slightly crumpled from being in his jacket pocket so long.

'My resignation,' said Willi.

Breuer took the paper out of the envelope and read it through twice, just to be sure. He looked up at Willi and smiled. Now that Willi would be out of his hair forever, he felt an unexpected flush of affection. 'Well, Geismeier,' he said, 'you did some good work while you were here.' But when he searched his mind for one example, he couldn't come up with anything.

'So, what's next for you?' he said.

'Oh, you know, Captain. Spend more time with the family.'

The joke went over Breuer's head. 'Yes, right you are, Geismeier. That's the ticket.'

Back in his office, Willi unlocked his desk. He looked through one drawer after the other to make sure nothing but departmental business was left behind. From the center drawer, he took out a thick file labeled *Krosius*. He leafed through it – copies of bank documents, photos, Joachim's drawings, his own notes, and a small coil of blue yarn. Like Elke, he kept it as a token, and he wasn't about to throw it away now. Then he put the file in his briefcase, locked the center drawer, tossed the keys on top of the desk, and went home.